THE REGATTA

MURDERS

ISBN: 9798519536479

First published 2021 by Follow This Publishing, Yorkshire (UK)
Text © 2021 Chris Turnbull
Cover Design © 2021 Joseph Hunt of Incredibook Design
Editor: Karen Sanders Editing

For Kate
Who has the warmest smile I know

Happy Reading !

C Turnbull
2024.

ALSO BY CHRIS TURNBULL

A Detective Matthews Novel

-2-

The Regatta Murders

Chris Turnbull

"Misfortunes one can endure--they come from outside, they are accidents. But to suffer for one's own faults--ah!--there is the sting of life."
— **Oscar Wilde, Lady Windermere's Fan**

PROLOGUE

'You do know it's the bride who's supposed to make you wait, not the other way around, my friend?'

'Yes, yes. I'm ready now,' Detective Benjamin Matthews shouted down the stairs to his best man and oldest friend John Travers Cornwell, known to those closest to him as Jack. Matthews caught a final glance at himself in the free-standing mirror, an old thing that was rusting slightly in the corners. His bright green eyes and slicked back chestnut brown hair gazed back at him. He was clean-shaven as always, and his tall, lean figure meant he had to bend down to see himself entirely in the reflection. He

1

straightened his tie and adjusted the cufflinks his father had given to him, scintillating silver and oval-shaped with such a beautifully hand-engraved pattern; worn by his father at his own wedding. Satisfied with his attire and taking a deep breath to suppress the nerves, he finally made to leave his bedroom.

'Matthews!' Jack shouted up the stairs again, anxiously looking at his watch every couple of seconds.

'I'm here,' Matthews replied as he marched down the staircase. 'Do you have the ring?'

'What ring?' Jack teased, a smirk across his face. 'Of course I do.' Jack pulled out a ring box from within his jacket pocket to prove he wasn't prevaricating. 'Now, can we go, please?'

'Yes!' Matthews scowled, though a grin soon followed. He had been waiting for this day for what felt like a lifetime, and now it had finally arrived he was encountering unexpected nerves. He wondered if she was feeling them too.

He locked his front door, and together they began walking to the church. The sky above Whitby was bright blue, although there was still a slight nip in the air, causing their breath to be visible with every exhale. The heat from the sun was finally warming again after a long, cold winter. Whitby was known for them, especially with the cold winds that blew down from the arctic and in from the North Sea.

From his townhouse on E Crescent, it was a short walk down to the harbour. They took a shortcut through a narrow passage, emerging by the riverside. The sounds and smells of the fishing boats and loading bays along the riverside could be overwhelming at times, but to the locals, this was the beating heart of Whitby. Always full of noise and activity, yet full of charm. Matthews was a familiar face with most of the locals, and today of all days, he could barely walk a handful of steps without more of them wishing him well. Whether it be approaching him to shake his hand or shouting out to him from across the street. Not only had his father, the chief of police, been proudly telling everybody and anybody who would listen it was his son's wedding day, but he'd also been surprised to see a small mention in the local newspaper. The heading of the piece read 'Police Chief's Eldest Son to Marry on Wednesday.' Why it was newsworthy was baffling to Matthews, yet in a remote town like Whitby, the smallest of things became well known to all.

'So, when are you going to let me be your best man? You've been calling on Miss Pilling for several months now,' Matthews challenged as they crossed the swing bridge to the East Cliff side of town.

'Soon, my friend.' Jack laughed. 'I think we both know she's not a patient woman and will expect that ring on her finger before the year is out.'

'A woman who knows what she wants. I admire her for that. No wonder she gets on so well with my soon-to-be wife.' Matthews chuckled.

Matthews and Jack had been friends since their school days. When Jack returned to town after serving in the navy and Matthews returned from working in York, the two men had been inseparable. Despite being the same age, Jack looked much older. His thick, unruly beard, wiry hair, and tired face made him look twice the detective's age. They were both tall, yet Jack had much broader shoulders and more muscular. He had bright blue eyes that stood out against his dark beard and pale skin.

The two men made their way along the cobbles of Church Street, consumed by their conversation.

Upon returning to Whitby last year, Matthews had been devising a plan to leave the town from day one. Although he still missed the bigger city and his job at the York police department, he felt more at home now with his fiancé, his family close by, and of course, his friends.

An almighty scream emanating from the market square and a woman shouting, 'Stop that boy,' interrupted their pleasant conversation.

Matthews turned to see a young boy, no older than twelve, running off in the opposite direction with a handful of items. Without thinking twice, Matthews took off after the boy.

'Matthews…' Jack shouted, '… your wedding!'

But it was too late. Matthews was already racing after the young boy through the square and onto the narrow street of Sandgate.

'Hey, you!' shouted Matthews. 'Boy!'

The youngster did not turn to see who was calling him and continued to run. Passers-by stumbled out of the way before being knocked flying by the young lad. Matthews, who was struggling to run his usual speed in his suit, was fearful he wouldn't catch up. The boy reached the busy swing bridge, which was always filled with horse and carts heading in different directions. The traffic slowed the boy somewhat, but unfortunately for Matthews, it slowed him too. As the boy turned left and ran up-river, Matthews spotted a uniformed officer and shouted for him to assist. The officer came charging towards Matthews and caught up to him quicker than expected. Together they raced along the riverside in chase of the boy. It looked as though they were about to snatch him, but the boy, in a desperate attempt to flee, jumped from the high quayside into the low-lying river below.

Matthews and the other officer arrived on the spot and looked down to see the young boy trying to swim, the items he had stolen floating behind him. Moments later, the boy was picked up by a passing boat, the owner of which also pulled in some of the floating objects. The boat owner had seen the entire event from the other side of the harbour and directed his boat back towards Matthews and the other waiting officer.

'Detective.' The vessel owner greeted him as though he knew him. 'I believe this is what you're after?' He handed up the young boy from the hull of the boat back up to the quayside. Before he could run off again, the uniformed officer grabbed hold of the young boy, placed him in handcuffs, and escorted him away.

'I can take these items back to the stallholder,' Matthews told the officer while collecting the items from the boatman. 'Though I don't know how well they'll sell now they're wet and smelly.' Matthews turned to leave with all the things in hand when confronted by an angry-looking Jack.

'I had one job, to get you to the church on time. If she's already there waiting for you, she'll string me up by my manhood.'

Matthews didn't reply but instead balanced the items in one arm and looked at his pocket watch; it was already two minutes past eleven. The ceremony was supposed to start two minutes ago.

'And look at your suit!' Jack roared. 'Those items are wet and dirty!' Without another word to one and another, the two men raced back across the swing bridge and along Church Street. Matthews quickly handed back the dirty items to the market stallholder and continued on before she could thank him. Already out of breath, they bolted up the one hundred and ninety-nine steps and did not stop until they'd reached the top; neither able to speak as they wheezed and gasped for air.

St Mary's Church looked picturesque against the blue sky, but Matthews and Jack didn't have time to stop and admire the views. They raced to the church doors, and as they were about the go inside, a horse and carriage pulled up beyond the graveyard, the ruins of Whitby Abbey in the distance behind the carriage. Matthews gave a sigh of relief; he hadn't kept her waiting.

Matthews and Jack brushed each other down in the church's doorway and straightened their ties. A final deep breath and they entered the chapel, walking down the aisle together. All eyes turned to look at them, many of which looking relieved to see them finally arrive. The first person Matthews spotted was his younger brother, Robert, his wife, Daniella, and their one-year-old daughter, May, sitting in the third row. They lived out of town, and Matthews saw them rarely.

In front of Robert was Matthews' sister, Charlotte, and her husband, John. Charlotte, who was over four months pregnant and already looked rather large-bellied, was already getting emotional at the sight of her older brother.

Finally at the front, Matthews and Jack had no time to speak as the organ began to play, and the congregation stood. Matthews kept his eyes forward for the time being, though he could sense everybody else in the room was looking back at the doors, waiting to see his bride. His heart was still beating out of its chest, and his mouth was dry and palms sweaty, though he knew it wasn't entirely due to the recent running.

He knew she must have walked in as whispers and gasps spread through the congregation. An uplifting feeling of joy and emotion emitted around the room. Even the vicar's face lit up with delight, letting Matthews know she was walking towards him. Matthews took a large gulp of air and turned around to view his bride walking towards him; his eyes visibly widened at the sight of her. Grace looked stunning in an oversized white ruffled dress and the most delicate veil you could see her smiling face through. Her blonde hair shone like the sun from beneath, and her striking blue eyes were fixated on him with every step she took towards him. Her father, a short bald dumpy man, led her up the aisle, his face glee-ridden.

Now by Matthews' side, Grace's father placed her hand into that of her new husband's. Her hand was as shaky as his. The organ fell silent, the congregation sat, and the ceremony began.

Chapter I

'I'm sorry, Mrs Ainley, but your son is dead.'

'Dead!' screeched Ainley. 'What do you mean he's dead? I called you here to help!' Mrs Ainley broke down into violent sobs, holding herself against a chair for support. The doctor helped her to sit down and handed her a handkerchief from his jacket pocket.

'My sincere condolences, Mrs Ainley, but there was nothing I could have done at this stage.' Doctor Bennett spoke in a calm, circumspect tone. He was known for his patience and composure. His well-spoken manner and kind nature made him one of the

11

top doctors in town. His old suits, which usually consisted of missing buttons or small frayed holes, were an amusement to people, given his known wealth. His wonky glasses balanced on the end of his nose, and his enormous bushy moustache was, without a doubt, his standout feature. 'I'm afraid it was too late for me to fully diagnose his condition. He was unresponsive when I arrived, and I was unable to conclude his ailment before his passing. If you'd like to know the cause of death, I can ask the coroner, Mr Waters, to conduct a post-mortem.'

'What... good... will... that... do?' Mrs Ainley said, her bottom lip quivering as she tried to keep it together. 'It's... not goin' to bring him back.' And she exuded into another fit of loud sobbing. Mrs Ainley was in her mid-forties, a widow, and lived in a rented room above a confectionery shop on Flowergate with her only son, Bert. Though not a wealthy woman, she always made sure she was smartly presented in her floor-length frocks, and her dark hair was perfectly styled into a bun on top of her head.

'No. I'm afraid it won't bring him back, Mrs Ainley, but a fit young man like your son shouldn't have just died all suddenly.'

'Are you…' she blew her nose on his handkerchief before continuing, '…saying you think he didn't die of natural cause? 'Cause if you're trying to pin the blame on my cookin', sir, I'll…'

'Madam, I am certainly not trying to blame you,' Doctor Bennett cut in. 'All I'm telling you is that it's extremely unusual for a healthy young man of eighteen years old to die so unexpectedly. If you would like him to be checked over, we can arrange that.'

Reluctant to leave her alone too quickly, Doctor Bennett made Mrs Ainley a hot drink and offered to get her something to eat. It was eight o'clock in the morning, and he had been there an hour already. Bert Ainley had been clinging to life when the doctor had arrived just before seven o'clock, but before he had even had the chance to thoroughly examine the young man, he had died in his own bed. His athletic body was weak and pale.

'Mrs Ainley, I need to get a message to the coroner to collect your son's body. I will step out for a moment, but I promise to return.' Mrs Ainley simply nodded, and the doctor left the first-floor bedsit and returned to the quiet street below.

Mrs Ainley stood with a wobble and brushed herself down. She took a deep breath and headed for the curtain that concealed her son's bed. With a slight hesitation, she pulled back the drape and immediately broke down into tears once more. Her son lay there motionless on the bed, his pale torso and sunken face almost unrecognisable to her. He had dark circles around his eyes, and his body was soddened with sweat. He had always been so blithe and high-spirited, so to see him like this was torture to her. Sitting next to him on the bed, she took hold of his hand and gave it a squeeze; her sobbing continued.

Minutes later, Doctor Bennett returned to find Mrs Ainley laid on the bed next to her son, her arm around him as though he was a young boy again, being soothed to sleep. Doctor Bennett could hear her sobs from the stairwell. Unsure if she had heard him re-enter the room, he cleared his throat before speaking. She turned her head back in his direction, though her gaze never left her son.

'The coroner has been sent for, Mrs Ainley.' She did not acknowledge him and continued to embrace her lifeless son. 'If there's nothing more I can do for you, then I'll leave you in peace.' The doctor collected his bag from beside the bed and made to leave.

'Wait,' croaked Mrs Ainley. The doctor stood in the doorway and waited to hear her say more. 'I think you may be right, Doctor.' Bennett returned to the bedside, and Mrs Ainley sat upright.

'Right about what, ma'am?'

'About my son needing to be looked over. He said something to me yesterday, but I just thought he was trying to get out of helping me with the chores, and he'd always make excuses for not going to church on Sunday.'

'What was it he said to you?'

'He said he thought he'd been poisoned. But I said, 'who the hell would want to poison you?' It's not like we have much, you know. I told him he must've eaten something bad; he was complaining about stomach pains. That's why I panicked when you got here, Doc. I thought you might accuse me of feeding him something wrong.'

'Now, now, Mrs Ainley. Nobody will accuse you of doing anything of the sort. But if what you tell me is true, then I'll have to inform the police department. Poisoning is a criminal offence, and the coroner should be able to detect whether that's the case.'

'Please don't inform the police just yet, Doctor. I don't want our name dragged through the mud if it doesn't need to be.'

'I'm afraid, madam, I may have no choice. I will also inform the coroner of this update, see if there's anything he can do.'

'If you must report this to the police, then please can you only tell Detective Matthews.'

'Do you know him?'

'I've never met him, but I've seen him around town many times. They write about him in the newspaper a lot. Comes across as a nice man. I trust him not to go around telling every Tom, Dick, and Harry my business.'

'As you wish, Mrs Ainley. He attends the same Sunday service as my wife and me. I'll pass him a note confidentially. Though he will probably wish to speak with you.'

'I ain't got nothing to say.'

'I suggest you don't touch any of Bert's belongings either; the detective may wish to look through them himself.'

'Why? What would Bert have to hide in here?'

'He possibly doesn't, Mrs Ainley, but best not to

touch any of his belongings until Matthews gets here.'

Mrs Ainley grudgingly nodded.

With that, the doctor left, and Mrs Ainley found herself unsure what to do with herself. It was nearly an hour later that the coroner arrived with a horse and cart. At the sight of the empty wooden coffin being carried into her home by three large men, she again erupted into a flood of tears. She watched as they respectfully placed her son into the coffin and fixed the lid on top. Mr Waters, an elderly gentleman with bright white hair, gave his condolences. He told Mrs Ainley she was welcome to visit her son's body the following day and left her alone. Ainley watched from her window as the two horses marched back along the road, carrying the now occupied coffin away. Many passers-by watched from the street, and Mrs Ainley quickly stepped back from the window. Upon realising, several of them looked up at her.

***

Doctor Bennett arrived at St Mary's Church moments before the service was about to start. Although it was Sunday, he had had a busy morning visiting patients throughout the town and was worried he would miss the service altogether. As he and his wife took their seats towards the back, he browsed the congregation in the hope Detective Matthews was there; he was. The church was not the largest in town. Still, due to its location on top of the cliff, it was always the most popular. This weekly service seemed to be the week's top social event for some people. The church and grounds would often be a place for couples and families to catch up with friends and acquaintances after the service had finished, the higher class often using it for showing off their new hats and dresses. This, however, could not be said about everyone, and the doctor knew Detective Matthews was not one for hanging around to hear the local gossip. Nor was he one for idle chitchat, so Bennett knew he had to catch the detective before he disappeared.

'Erm, excuse me. Detective Matthews,' he hollered after him outside. He had spoken to the detective many times over the year, though only in a work manner.

'Ah, Doctor Bennett. How are you? You may not have met my wife; this is Grace. Grace, Doctor Bennett.' They exchanged pleasantries, and Bennett introduced them to his own wife. Matthews, presuming this to be a simple hello, steered his wife towards the one hundred and ninety-nine steps in order to leave.

'Begging your pardon, Detective. Could I have a quick word before you dash off?'

'Oh, of course.'

The doctor handed the detective an envelope with his name written on the front. 'Most of the details I've written down for you, but a Mrs Ainley sadly lost her son this morning, and she thinks it could have been a poisoning. Mr Waters has his body now, but Mrs Ainley wished for this to come directly to you. She's concerned about it becoming common gossip.' Doctor Bennett tried to keep his voice low as other members of the congregation passed them by.

'Thank you, Doctor Bennett. I'll look over this and pay a visit to Mr Waters tomorrow to see what, if anything, he's discovered.' Matthews and Grace wished the doctor and his wife a pleasant day and turned to leave.

'Oh, and Detective.' Matthews stopped and looked back. 'I would maybe suggest you speak to Mrs Ainley too. I get the most peculiar feeling she knows more than she's willing to admit.'

Chapter 2

Detective Benjamin Matthews took the long way to the station this morning, hoping the coastal breeze would help cool him down. The last few weeks had seen quite the heatwave in the town, causing most people to feel exhausted and sluggish throughout the day. It was barely eight o'clock, and the heat of the day was already increasing. The higher temperatures were also causing the town to smell much worse than it generally did, with the harbour reeking of rotten fish. The rest of the town was no better, with horse manure yet to be cleared from the street scenting the air. Even the sewage seemed to be extra fragrant these last couple of weeks.

On top of that, perspiring workers, and people in penury with no access to wash facilities made the town the smelliest Matthews had ever witnessed. He passed fishermen already hard at work on his way to the office, homeless children bathing in the water troughs designed for the many horses; even the seagulls spent more time on the water or in the shade than in the air these days. Despite the daily hardships some of these people had to deal with, the town always seemed upbeat.

However, this morning, Matthews had more of a skip in his step and was still floating on his recent good news. A week ago, Grace had been to the doctors and finally received the information they had been waiting for. They were going to have a baby. They had kept it to themselves for the remainder of the week and finally told Matthews' family at the dinner table yesterday. His father, the police chief, was ecstatic by the news and opened up a bottle of fizz to celebrate. Matthews' sister, Charlotte, was also excited. Even more so because she was due to give birth herself within the next couple of weeks. Matthews' younger brother, Robert, who already had an eighteen-month-old child, had not been there for dinner, so Matthews decided he would send word through during the week.

'Imagine that,' Matthews' father had exclaimed over dinner. 'Grandfather to not one, not two, but three grandchildren.' He poured the sparkling wine for all the men. 'Your mother would have been so proud of you all. A toast, to the next generation!' The rest of dinner had been hijacked by the talk of babies, though Matthews and Grace were so overjoyed, they didn't mind.

Knowing he would be a father was the most exciting thing in the world to him. As excited as he was, he couldn't help but feel a tinge of sadness that his mother was no longer around to meet her grandchildren. Matthews knew she would have made the best grandmother and would have already been fussing over them all.

Upon arriving at his office, Mrs Lloyd-Hughes, his secretary, was already in the outer office, tapping away on her typewriter. She was approaching fifty and had a greying bobbed haircut, and even in her small heels didn't quite reach the detective's shoulder.

'M-morning,' she croaked as Matthews

approached, though she didn't stop typing. 'M-mail's on your d-desk.' Her voice always sounded as though it was sore, and her stuttering was primarily due to her stifling a cough. She could often be heard coughing away between puffing her cigarettes, which she was usually surrounded by the smoke of. There was a large window next to her desk, which she'd opened as wide as possible in the expectation it would help mitigate the heat, though hardly any breeze pierced the first-floor office this morning, and she was visibly sweating.

'Thank you,' Matthews said before entering his office and also opening all the windows. Matthews, who always wore a waistcoat and shirt, removed the waistcoat and opened his shirt's top two buttons. He would normally wear a tie for work but had decided against this due to the heat. He checked his pocket watch, initially his grandfather's, which he'd inherited after his passing, and finally took a seat behind his large wooden desk.

There were three letters there waiting for him, one of which was from the coroner, Mr Waters, asking if he would be available to come and see him around four o'clock. Matthews knew immediately this would be regarding the young man Doctor Bennett had spoken to him about and left the open letter on the side of his desk as a reminder.

The second letter was from one of the station officers, letting Matthews know that a man he'd arrested last week had finally admitted to his crime. Matthews had been investigating a house fire for the previous two weeks. The occupant had been adamant it had been arson. At the end of last week, Matthews had had enough evidence to make an arrest.

As Matthews ripped open the third and final letter, in ran Harvey, the young assistant Matthews had been assigned last year. A year on and Harvey was no longer a stable hand that followed Matthews around but was now a junior officer. At only sixteen years old, he was still under the care of Matthews. Although Matthews always preferred to work alone, he had to admit that the second pair of hands had been helpful on numerous occasions throughout the year.

'Mornin', Detective.' Harvey bounced into the room. 'Any news on last week's arrest?' Harvey had been there for the whole investigation and was always keen to know any follow up information. Matthews passed him the letter to read. 'Brilliant. Told ya it was 'im all the time.'

'You are certainly getting a good instinct for this kind of thing. Though you still need to slow down a little. Just because we know who we think did something doesn't mean we can go all in until we can prove it. Unfortunately, a gut instinct isn't enough.'

'Yeah, yeah.' Harvey laughed and took the hard wooden seat opposite Matthews. 'So what we working on next?'

Harvey was a tall skinny lad with a pale complexion. Once covered in dirt, he was now neat and respectable in his junior officer's uniform. He had a thick head of messy brown hair, sleepy-looking dark eyes, and a smile that was both warm and cheeky.

'Well, I've still got to finish the report on the arson, and then this has just come through, though I'm not sure if it will lead to anything yet.' He handed over the letter he had received yesterday from Doctor Bennett.

'A Bert Ainley died. Do ya know 'im?' asked Harvey.

'No. I'm led to believe he lived with his mother on Flowergate. I have a note from Mr Waters asking me to see him later today, so once I know his opinion, I'll know whether to take it further.'

'Want me to come?'

'Not this time, but I'll let you know tomorrow if there's anything.' Matthews was speaking while scanning the third letter. It was from his old friend Jack, inviting him and Grace around for a celebratory drink this coming weekend. He had finally proposed to Miss Elizabeth Pilling. He wished for Matthews to be his best man.

'What you smiling at?' Harvey quizzed.

'Jack has finally proposed.'

'Oh, right. He was ya best man, wasn't he?'

'He was indeed, and it looks as though I'm returning the favour.' A smile crept out from the side of his face. He was genuinely happy for his friend.

***

It was late afternoon when Detective Matthews arrived at the coroner's office. Mr Waters was already outside the front door, smoking a cigar, waiting for him. He was an elderly man with a head full of bright white hair that was always messy and windswept. Though frail-looking at times, he was relatively fit for his age and seemed to be in no rush to retire. He was always clean-shaven, with large unruly sideburns that looked like an extension to his messy hair. He would always be in a clean-cut suit with a white cotton pleated shirt, and a black cravat, despite the time of year. His sunken, small, dark eyes reminded Matthews of a mole.

'Good afternoon, Detective. It's been a while since I last saw you.' Mr Waters smiled, revealing his crooked yellowing teeth.

'It certainly has been a while.' Matthews sighed. 'The last several months have been largely petty crimes for me. I did have a disappearance case a couple of weeks back, but it turned out he just wanted to leave his wife and failed to tell her.'

'I see.' Mr Waters chuckled. 'The poor woman.'

'Indeed.' Matthews allowed himself to find the funny side of it too, though the wife had not had the same reaction when Matthews had told her. 'Anyway, I got your message. What's the update on young Mr Ainley?' Matthews took out a notepad and pencil from his satchel, ready to make notes.

'I'm afraid, Detective, there's very little to tell you. Although he was a young, healthy man, or at least that's what Bennett tells me, he seems to have very few tell-tale signs as to what happened to him.' Mr Waters took another drag of his cigar. 'I'm sorry, would you like one?' He offered Matthews a smoke. The detective declined a cigar, though took out one of his own smaller cigarettes.

'So you don't think there's anything to investigate here?' Matthews placed the notepad back into his bag.

'Something I did think was odd is that his stomach was completely empty. Even people who have vomited usually have something in there. So either he hadn't eaten in days, or what he was eating was being vomited back up quicker than he could digest.'

'And you think this is suspicious enough for me to look into?'

'Bert Ainley had nothing I could find that would indicate he died from any illness. There were no signs on his body of bruising or flesh wounds, and his internal organs, though pale from his sickness and vomiting, all looked as though they should have been in working order.' Mr Waters gave an almighty cough as he finished speaking.

'Doctor Bennett said the boy's mother mentioned

poisoning. Can you see anything to show that?'

'Poisoning would indicate him being given something against his will, be that in his food or drink or injected into him. If he was injected, you would expect to see signs of a struggle, yet his body was free from bruises and cuts. As the stomach was empty, it's difficult to say what was there a day or two before. That amount of vomiting would likely remove any poisoned item. His blood did have a chemical reaction when tested, but again, I couldn't conclude poison as a definitive cause of death.'

'Though you wouldn't rule it out?'

'The boy looked to be in top physical health.' Waters gave out another phlegm ridden cough. 'People don't just drop dead as you well know. Nonetheless, my methods are good, but they cannot solve everything. That's where your work is still valuable. As I said, his blood did have a positive reaction to toxins, but I can't identify what that was exactly. If Bert Ainley died from poisoning, then he either knew the poisoner and took it willingly, or he was given it unbeknown to himself.'

'Thank you.' Matthews shook the coroner's hand. 'This could end up being nothing to investigate. But

I'll need to speak with his mother if she's claiming poison.'

CHAPTER 3

TUESDAY 2ND AUGUST 1892

Matthews had been reluctant to leave for work this morning because Grace had been up most of the night ill. He had felt helpless watching her suffer so greatly and wished he could have done something more to support her. Finally, at about three o'clock this morning, she had settled in to sleep, though Matthews was still on edge for the remainder of the night. An unused bedpan was placed beside the bed, should she be sick again.

'Are you sure you don't want me to ask Charlotte to come over today? She'll be able to give you some advice as her morning sickness was terrible at the beginning too.'

'Honestly, please stop worrying and go to work. I'll be okay. If I get tired, I will take a break. It's you I'm most worried about, going to work on such little sleep.' Even when tired and unwell, Grace thought of others before herself; this was one of the main attributes Matthews fell in love with her for. She was still in her nightgown, had no make-up on, and her golden hair loosely tumbled around her shoulders and down her back. To Matthews, she looked beautiful.

'Okay, but I will pop in to check on you.'

'Would you mind sending word to Joan that I'm coming in later today? Tell her I'll be in for lunchtime.' Joan was her boss at the dress shop.

'Certainly.' Matthews smiled. He was thrilled she was taking the morning more leisurely. And with that, he kissed her before leaving the house. Grace walked to the large front window that flooded the living room with light and gave him a wave. She knew she would be okay, and once her husband was out of sight, she headed back upstairs to wash and dress for the day.

***

Matthews couldn't relax all morning. After

sending Harvey to deliver a letter to Mrs Ainley requesting an interview, the rest of his morning was filled with completing the arson report. It was another blistering day, which was not helping Matthews with his concentration at all. He regularly checked his pocket watch, wondering when would be an appropriate time to go home and check Grace was still okay. He knew she would disapprove if he returned too soon. She was extraordinarily headstrong and was undoubtedly unlike most of the other wives in the town. She worked for a local dressmaker and was getting a name for herself, making some of the most beautiful outfits in the town. She even made her own clothes and had started to make shirts and suits for Matthews. He decided he would leave before lunch. If she was determined to make it into work for the afternoon shift, he would at least get a carriage and give her a lift there.

'Morning, son. How's that report coming along?' His father, Chief David Matthews', booming voice made him jump. He was a larger than life kind of man, whose loud voice and laughter was distinguishable in a crowd.

'Almost finished,' Matthews lied.

'And how's Grace doing? Busy planning for the new arrival, I suppose?'

Matthews could tell his father was just as excited about becoming a grandfather again as Matthews was about being a father.

'Indeed. Already looking at fabrics for baby outfits. She's already started some for Charlotte's pending arrival too. Maybe Charlotte will pass them on when hers outgrows them.' Matthews put down his pencil, leant his elbows on the desk, and rubbed his tired eyes.

'Everything all right?' the chief asked, leaning against the vacant chair opposite Matthews.

'Grace was quite unwell overnight. I'll probably shoot back at some point to check on her.'

'Yes, yes. Earns you brownie points with the missus too. You know, your mother suffered terribly with all three of you, yet she was still determined to have you all. After two boys, I thought she would say enough, but she was desperate for a girl. Thank goodness the third one was a girl, or I'm sure she would have had me keep going until we had one.' The chief snorted with laughter. 'Anyway, you should ask Charlotte what she did for the sickness. I don't think she has it as bad anymore.'

'I think I'll ask her to come around for a visit and casually drop it into the conversation; that way, Grace won't think I'm trying to control the situation. She seems to think she doesn't need help.'

'Strong headed women for you. Head on to the pharmacy. They might have something worth taking. Anyway, I only wanted to pop my head in. I'll see you later.' With that, the chief made to leave.

'Oh, by the way,' said Matthews, 'Jack has finally proposed to Beth.'

'"Bout bloody time if you ask me.' And he left the office, chuckling to himself.

It was now approaching midday, and Matthews was putting the final touches to his report before heading home to check on Grace.

'D-Detective…' came Mrs Lloyd-Hughes' voice from the doorway. 'Y-You h-have a v-visitor.'

Matthews looked up in time to see a woman in her mid-forties walk into the room. She was well-presented, with dark hair tied up tightly into a bun, though she looked rather put out to be here.

'Detective Matthews, my name is Mrs Ainley.' She took a seat opposite him. 'I got your letter, asking for a conversation. Shall we get this over with straight away?'

Matthews was a little taken aback. He hadn't even had time to prepare what he was going to ask her.

'Oh… well, of course.' He found himself checking his pocket watch again. Grace would be leaving for work in an hour.

'It's only if this meeting was hanging over my head for too long, I'd go crackers, so I thought best to just get it over and done with.' In her all-black dress with her swollen eyes, it was evident Mrs Ainley was grieving. Matthews could sense she was trying her hardest to put on a brave face.

'Mrs Ainley, how old was your son?' Matthews scrambled for his notepad.

'Eighteen/ Would have turned nineteen next month.'

'Did he work?'

'Oh, yes. As a labourer. Been there since he was young. His father used to work there before he passed.'

'Could I get the details? I may need to pay them a visit.'

'I'm not sure off the top of my head, but I'll

probably have something at home. I wouldn't put it past that lot being behind this. I told my husband I didn't want Bert working there, and now look what's happened.'

'May I ask what you mean by that, Mrs Ainley? You dislike his co-workers?'

'All a bunch of scoundrels if you ask me.' She scowled. 'Wouldn't trust a single one of them. Probably one of them who's responsible for my Bert's...' Her voice trembled as she spoke. 'The place is full of petty criminals. Just get yourself up there, Detective, I'm sure the culprit who poisoned my son will be there.'

'Thank you,' Matthews responded while taking notes. 'I'll come by for that information later. An address of the yard or name of the foreman; anything really will be a help.' Matthews made a note of it. 'Mrs Ainley, moving on, would you say your son was healthy? Did he look after himself?' Matthews was so utterly thrown by her unexpected arrival that he was worried he would forget to ask something important. He usually had a little more time to prep questions before an interview.

'He was always doing sit-ups and press-ups in the

living room. His job was physical, you see, so it built up muscle naturally.' Mrs Ainley took out a tissue from her handbag and wiped the tears from her eyes. 'He wasn't huge, but he certainly liked to think he was muscular. He joined the Friendship Rowing Club when he was sixteen and would usually be down there at least once a week. He said he liked the chaps who did it. I know he also enjoyed the exercise and took his physical appearance seriously. On a hot day, he would be the first one at work to take his shirt off. Got himself in trouble a couple of times for it. Well... it's not appropriate, is it?'

'Mrs Ainley, when did your son first show signs he was unwell?'

'Bert went out for drinks with some work friends on the Thursday night. They normally wait until the weekend, but I think it was a birthday or something. Anyway, he came home rather drunk, and I had to look after him and put him into bed. We live in a bedsit, you see, so there's no way he can sneak in without me hearing him.'

'And he was unwell from then on?'

'The day after, he was feeling rough, though he did get out of bed, but he didn't go to work. I just blamed a hangover. He decided not to have any food as he was convinced he was going to be sick. That night, and into Saturday morning, he seemed to get worse and developed sweats. I was still saying it was the alcohol and tried to look after him myself. He was sick a few times but didn't really settle all night.' Mrs Ainley paused to wipe her eyes again. 'I kept trying to get fluids into him, but even that he couldn't keep down. Then the whole of Saturday, he just stayed in bed. He looked pale but was talking. I told him off for getting so drunk, but he said he thought it was more than that. Said he thought he'd been poisoned.'

'Did he give any indication who he thought might have poisoned him?'

'No, but in truth, I didn't take it too seriously. Bert was saying all kinds of things in the end. Delusional he was.'

'When did you call for the doctor?'

'On Saturday night. He seemed more settled, though he again refused to eat all day despite my many attempts to make him. I went to bed and thought he was having a more peaceful night, though when I woke up at about five o'clock, I decided to check on him, and he looked dead. I started to shake him, and he came around, though he wasn't making any sense. I eventually got a message to the doctor, who arrived a little before seven o'clock, but it was too late. Bert died within minutes of him arriving.' She held her handkerchief up to her face and began to sob. After a couple of seconds, she took in a deep breath and tried to get herself together.

'Thank you for re-telling that, Mrs Ainley. I'm sure it wasn't easy for you.' Matthews was trying to think if there was anything more he needed to know. It was often the case that follow-up interviews had to be taken. The doctor had mentioned to Matthews that he suspected Mrs Ainley was keeping something to herself, and now talking to her himself, Matthews felt the same.

'Finally, is there anything else you think I should know?'

Mrs Ainley looked somewhat taken aback by this question. 'I don't think so.' She sniffed, all the while not looking at the detective.

'Mrs Ainley, it would be useful for me to visit your home and look through your son's personal belongings. Have you touched anything since his death?'

'The doctor told me not to.'

'Very good.' Matthews examined his pocket watch. He was now too late to see Grace; she would have left for work already. 'Would you be happy for me to accompany you back now? I could check Bert's belongings and you can see if you have the information on his employer.'

Mrs Ainley was clearly trying to keep a straight face and failing badly. Matthews wondered if she had come to his office purposefully so the detective could not look through her son's belongings.

'Of course, Detective.' Mrs Ainley gave a weak smile. 'Let me lead the way.'

CHAPTER 4

Matthews left a note with Mrs Lloyd-Hughes for Harvey just in case he came back and wondered where he had gone. He gave her his finished report for the arson case and asked her politely if she would mind submitting it for him while he was out. She gladly agreed while balancing a cigarette in her mouth and tapping on the typewriter at the same time.

Stepping back out into the early afternoon heat, Matthews found it challenging to concentrate on Mrs Ainley's ramblings.

'I told my Gerald it was a bad idea to get him a job there, but would he listen? Would he hell,' she told the detective as they walked along the street together. 'He's been there about four years now, and never have I liked any of them. Not that I've met many of them, mind, but Gerald always had a story to tell when he got home. God bless his soul.' She sniffed, and Matthews thought she was about to cry again.

'How long has your husband been dead, Mrs Ainley?'

'Be just over two years now.' She sighed. 'Gosh, don't the time fly by? I remember our wedding like it was yesterday, though that would have been twenty years next spring.'

They made it onto Flowergate, which was now busy with traders and shoppers alike. It was a quieter street than some of the others in town, but a lot wider, too, which was a novelty for most shopping streets.

'Do you work, Mrs Ainley?' Matthews asked as they reached the street-side door up to the bedsit.

'Do I?' She gave out a laugh. 'I couldn't afford to live here if I didn't. My husband was a good man, but he left nothing behind for me to live off when he passed.' She led the detective upstairs into the tiny living quarters. 'Sorry 'bout the mess,' she said sheepishly as she closed the door behind them.

'Not at all,' Matthews replied. 'You have a lovely home.' In truth, there was a distinct smell about the place that was unpleasant. Her small kitchenette had washing piled on the floor and dirty dishes in the sink, and the chopped vegetable peelings on the side were beginning to rot.

There were two worn armchairs beside a small wood burner littered in ash and a small round kitchen table between them and the kitchenette.

On the other side of the bedsit was a curtain set that Matthews could already see separated two beds.

'Bert's bed was through there.' Mrs Ainley pointed towards the curtains, and Matthews headed through to take a look. It was rather dark in the back of the bedsit, but Mrs Ainley was already one step ahead and, seconds later, followed him into the curtained area with a lit candle. 'I'll leave you this.' She placed it on the bedside table. 'Wanna drink?'

'No, thank you. I shouldn't keep you long.'

Mrs Ainley left the bedroom area and retired to one of the armchairs. Matthews was consciously aware that she was watching his every move.

Bert's curtained-off bedroom area was relatively

modest, with a single bed that looked as though it hadn't been touched since Bert had laid in it. Matthews checked the bedside table, and other than a few personal items, found nothing of importance. He then began moving the small wooden bedside table to look under and behind it. Having searched many rooms before, Matthews knew all the tricks. As he pushed this to look behind, he could hear Mrs Ainley shuffling uncomfortably from the sitting area. She was trying to see what the detective was doing.

'Everything all right?' she eventually hollered.

'Yes, thank you,' Matthews replied, and once happy there was nothing there, placed the furniture back into position.

Under the bed was a large trunk and nothing else except a bedpan. Matthews pulled out the chest and opened it up on top of the bed. The contents were a mixture of clothes and personal items such as newspaper clippings and magazines about sport, rowing, and fitness. Matthews was about to place the trunk away when something on one of Bert's shirts caught his eye. It looked as though something had spilt onto the shirt, though the detective couldn't identify what it could have been. Furthermore, the stain was still relatively damp.

'Mrs Ainley, did you say you hadn't touched any of your son's belongings since his passing?'

'No, Detective. Doctor Bennett told me I best not.'

'And you made sure to follow those instructions?'

'Of course. Why? Is everything okay?' Her voice carried through the bedsit, but surprisingly to Matthews, she did not come and see what the issue could be. Matthews checked through the bedding and under the mattress, and nothing seemed out of sorts. With nothing else in the curtained-off bedroom, he left the bedside and returned to the seating area.

'Mrs Ainley, would you mind if I checked the rest of your home just in case Bert placed something in a different area?' Matthews asked, watching her reaction closely.

'If you think it will help, Detective, but I assure you there is nothing here. I don't understand what you think you'll find. It's his work colleagues you need to be checking with; they'll be the ones with something to hide.'

'Do you have their details?'

'Let me see now.' She walked over to the

kitchenette and pulled open one of the drawers. 'Handwritten payslip here has the company name and foreman's name on it. Will that help?'

'Indeed it will. Thank you, Mrs Ainley.' Matthews took the payslip and placed it into his satchel. After a quick swoop of the bedsit, Matthews was unsurprised not to find anything of interest. Eventually, he thanked her for her time and informed her he'd be in touch should anything come up. A few moments later, the detective was back out on Flowergate. Though he couldn't prove anything, he perceived that Mrs Ainley had been hiding something, but what? She seemed adamant that the men at the building yard were to blame for her son's death, so he knew visiting them would be the next thing on his agenda.

Headed back to the station, Matthews decided to take a detour and pay a quick visit to Grace's dress shop. The owner was an older woman named Joan, a part of Whitby's fashion scene since before Matthews was born. His mother used to get her dresses from Joan, and Charlotte was a fan of the shop too.

'What are you doing here?' Grace's face lit up at the sight of him entering the store.

'Can't a husband surprise his wife with a passing

hello?' He now wished he'd picked up some flowers on the way. The shop floor was empty, and Grace had been dressing a mannequin in a half-finished dress. He strode over to her and kissed her.

'Careful.' She laughed. 'I have pins sticking out everywhere!'

'Well, that's a new excuse for trying to stab your husband. I've never heard that one before.' They both laughed, and she leaned in to kiss him again.

'What's all this commotion?' Joan appeared from the backroom. She was a well-dressed larger woman in her early eighties. Her grey hair was large and over the top, just like her fabric choice, and she wore many necklaces that glistened in the light. 'Oh, Detective. It's you.' She walked around the counter, and he gave her a peck on the cheek.

'No Beth today?' Matthews inquired.

'She does mornings on Tuesday,' Grace replied. 'Though she told me the news. I believe we're going for dinner at the weekend.'

'Indeed.' Matthews smirked. 'Anyway, I better let you get on before you stick more pins in me.' The three of them laughed.

'It was lovely seeing you, Detective,' Joan called as

she headed back into the other room.

'Likewise,' Matthews shouted after her.

'I'll see you at home then?' Grace turned back to her mannequin.

'Or maybe I'll come back and walk you home.' Matthews kissed her on the cheek then headed for the door.

'Scared I'll get lost, Mr Matthews?' He smirked at her comment, and she blew him a kiss before he left the shop.

Outside the shop and back under the heat of the blistering sun, Matthews took out Bert Ainley's payslip. He recognised the name of the building yard immediately; it was one of the largest in town. He also knew the foreman by name, but not in a favourable way. The detective knew this was an odious man, yet this, of course, wasn't proof he had anything to do with Mr Ainley's death. Matthews began to walk back to the station, his mind so full of thoughts that he almost walked into a passing woman. He couldn't let go of the belief that Mrs Ainley was hiding something.

CHAPTER 5

'So you're closing the case?' the chief asked for the second time. His booming voice was even more shocked than the first time he'd said it.

'I don't see any other option,' Matthews replied, tidying away the papers on his desk so he could get ready to go home. 'Mrs Ainley swears she didn't touch anything in their bedsit, and there was nothing solid to indicate any wrongdoing.'

'But Mr Waters…'

'Mr Waters said he couldn't find anything to prove Bert Ainley had been poisoned. His hunch that he must have been given something is not conclusive enough evidence.'

'And you have followed every possible lead?'

'Pops, there is not enough evidence in his body, in his home, and no motives to want Bert Ainley dead. So unless you can see something I'm missing, then please can you let me get on.' Matthews was trying to stop himself from raising his voice. His relationship with his father had never been the smoothest, but the last thing he wanted was another row.

'It just seems like there should be something more to this.' The chief spoke softly, a contrast to his usual deep booming voice, and stood up ready to leave.

'I agree.' Matthews sighed. 'It's like an unsolved puzzle, and you know how they drive me mad.'

'Did you speak to his employer?'

'Yesterday. A Mr Talbot, who hires numerous young men for various paid labour work around town. It's cash in hand for most of them, and he didn't even remember who Bert was. One of his colleagues spoke to me, confirming that Bert had been out drinking in the middle of the week, as Mrs Ainley had mentioned. Said he didn't see anything unusual at the time. He did mention that Bert had been acting fatigued that week, but they'd been doing heaving lifting for a fortnight, and they were all exhausted.'

'Has the mother arranged a funeral for her son?'

'I believe it's due to take place at the end of next week, though it was Mr Waters who mentioned that to me.'

'Well, I'll let you leave. I'm sure you're looking forward to getting home. Do give Grace my regards.'

'Thanks, Pop. We're seeing Jack and Beth this evening. I'm expecting him to ask me to be his best man.' Matthews smirked to himself as he said this.

'Ah, fantastic.' The chief's booming tone had returned. 'Do pass on my congratulations.' And with that, the chief left the office.

It was now a couple of minutes past six o'clock, and the summer sun was still relatively high in the sky. The heatwave was continuing, and Matthews found himself exhausted as he tidied his desk before leaving for the day. He wished he could just go home and relax with his wife for the evening instead of going out.

Grace had still been suffering a lot with morning sickness. Yet, although she was struggling, she still managed to keep a positive attitude and had continued to make it into work each day. Matthews was in admiration of her and felt dreadful every morning when he had to leave. This morning had seen one of her worst plights of sickness, to the point that Matthews nearly called for the doctor. Grace, however, had refused him to do so and eventually made it back to bed. These restless nights not only affected Grace, but Matthews found himself unable to sleep, even after she had drifted off. He wasn't sure how either of them would cope for the remainder of the pregnancy.

Upon arriving home around half-past six, Matthews was delighted by the sight of Grace in the sitting room. She was wearing a stunning burnt orange floor-length gown with puff sleeves, a laced front, and a high collar. Her blonde hair was primarily styled up with a couple of loose strands around her ears.

'You look beautiful.' Matthews embraced her.

'Are you ready to leave?' Grace asked, using her hand to brush his shirt and waistcoat.

'Give me two minutes to change my shirt, and I'll be ready.'

It was seven o'clock when they finally arrived outside Jack's quaint stone-built cottage on Arundel Place. One of a row of identical cottages that sat on a quiet back street behind Arundel manor house. Matthews had been a regular visitor over the past year, especially at Jack's poker nights.

'Are you sure you're feeling up for this?' Matthews asked, conscious of how unwell Grace had been that morning.

'Certainly. Getting out of the house is exactly what I need.' She squeezed his hand and kissed his cheek. 'If I start to feel uneasy, I'll let you know.' As Matthews exited and turned to help Grace out the carriage door, he could already hear his friend's voice coming from the cottage doorway.

'Hurry up and get inside, Mutton. The neighbours will think you're here to arrest me.' Jack gave a chuckle and instantly pulled his friend into an embrace. He had reverted to calling Matthews, Mutton, from time to time in jest. Taken from the phrase Mutton-shunter, a common term for a police officer. 'Grace, you're looking beautiful as ever.' He kissed her hand. 'How this so-called gentleman convinced you to marry him I will never know.' He gave out a deep throaty laugh, jabbing Matthews in the ribs with his elbow.

'Good evening, Jack.' Grace laughed. 'Always a pleasure.' Jack showed them through to the sitting room, where Beth was already pouring drinks. 'Beth, it's so good to see you. Have you been here long?' Grace instantly greeted their host.

'I arrived this afternoon with mother. You know what she's like. Couldn't possibly leave me alone with a man until I'm married. She helped me do the cooking; only left about a minute ago herself.' Elizabeth Pilling, or Beth, as most of her friends called her, was extremely pale with strawberry blonde hair. She was the thinnest woman Matthews had ever met, yet somehow always managed to be seen eating at gatherings. She was not shy and was always chatty in her girlish voice. Beth had the most hypnotic hazel eyes that felt as though they looked into you and the warmest smile that made you believe as though you'd known her all your life. Despite her petite frame, she was anything but weak. She stood up for what she believed in and was not afraid to speak up. This is what Jack had loved about her the most. Matthews and Grace had to admit they admired this about her too. She worked at the same dress shop in town as Grace and had met Jack through her. Beth had never hidden her feelings about Jack, and from the moment she met him, she was more than open about the fact she wished to be married and have children.

Excited by their guests' arrival, Beth took Grace by the hand and gave her a kiss on the cheek. 'Your dress is beautiful, Grace. Did you make it yourself?'

'I did.' Grace replied. 'It was mostly old cuts from other dresses, but it turned out better than expected.' Beth ran her hands along the fabric.

'Oh, of course. I saw you working on it during your lunch breaks but didn't realise it was for yourself. That colour is stunning on you.'

'Thank you.' Grace blushed. 'I'd best enjoy it whilst I can. Now I'm pregnant, it won't be long before I no longer fit in it.'

'I can help you alter some of your dresses if you'd like. It will be good practise for when I have to do my own.' She giggled and looked at her fiancé. Jack was talking to Matthews and pretending he hadn't heard.

Beth had spent the afternoon preparing a wonderful meal for them all, and after their initial pleasantries, invited Matthews and Grace through to the dining table. Having worked together for nearly a year, Grace and Beth had become good friends, and Grace would not take no for an answer when she offered Beth a helping hand in the kitchen.

'You must be excited about your upcoming wedding,' Grace mentioned excitedly. 'Have you picked a date yet?'

'We're hoping for September. We're going to see the vicar tomorrow.'

'Have you given any thought about your dress?'

'Well, actually, yes.' Beth stopped dishing up the dinner and turned to face Grace. Her expression turned serious. 'I was wondering, since you're so much better at it than me, if you'd be willing to help me make it?' She took a hold of her friends' hand, her expression nervous and her eyes wide in anticipation of Graces' reply.

'Of course I will.' Grace squealed with excitement and gave Beth a hug. 'We'll have to look at pattern designs next week. September is next month, so we don't have long.' They returned to the dining room, where Matthews and Jack were also in conversation about the wedding.

'Guess who has just agreed to be my best man?'

Jack asked Beth playfully.

'Oh, fantastic,' Grace said before excitedly telling her husband her own news.

The evening passed by in the blink of an eye. Beth's dinner of roasted fish and vegetables, and a delicious sponge cake for dessert, had gone down a storm. Grace took it easy on the portions, aware that she did not want to be overdoing it with such bad morning sickness. As Matthews and Grace prepared themselves to leave, there was a knock on the door.

'Probably our carriage driver. We had said for him to come around about this time,' Matthews told Jack.

'Could be my mother too,' Beth replied. 'She was determined to return to collect me.' Beth and Grace exchanged amused glances.

Matthews offered to answer the door. Ready to shout out, 'on our way out now,' to the carriage driver, he was stopped by the realisation it was not who he had been expecting.

'Harvey, what are you doing here?'

'Chief told me where to find ya.' He was breathing heavily, as though he'd been running. 'Needed ya to 'ave this note tonight'. Harvey handed over an envelope to the detective, his brow wet with sweat from the still warm evening. The carriage pulled up outside at that moment behind him.

'A note about what? What couldn't wait?'

'Mr Waters, the coroner requests to see you first thing in the morning. There's been another young man die, and it looks to be similar circumstances.'

CHAPTER 6

'Ha ow will you know if the two deaths are related?' Harvey asked, trying to keep up with the detective's long strides.

'Well, I'm hoping Mr Waters will confirm that part for us. We can then look into the rest.' Harvey had called at Matthews' house this morning so they could walk there together. Over the last year, Harvey had become a familiar figure beside the detective. Since becoming a junior officer, he had even been allowed to investigate or follow up some leads himself, though only with Matthews' permission.

They arrived at the coroner's shortly after eight o'clock in the morning. It was glorious out again and looked to be yet another scorching day ahead. Matthews preferred the summer months, though even he was getting a little exhausted by the heatwave. It felt as though it had been going on for months now, yet in truth, it must have only been a couple of weeks.

'Matthews!' greeted Mr Waters at the door. 'And you brought Harvey this time too. Getting taller every time I see you, young man.' Harvey smirked. It was true he was already taller than Mr Waters, though he would likely never be as tall as the detective, who stood well over a foot taller still.

Waters led them through to his office, a smallish room with a window that looked through to the autopsy room. Thankfully, there was nothing on display at the moment, to Harvey's liking. The office felt more like a broom cupboard, with a tiny desk compressed in, almost touching the walls on both sides, that Mr Waters had to scrape around to get to his seat. There was no natural light in the office at all, and Waters had to light many candles before they could begin. Behind the desk were shelves upon shelves of papers and files, which to the untrained eye looked to be just a pile of mess. His desk was no better, with paperwork littering it to the point that none of the surfaces was visible.

'It's pleasantly cool in here,' Matthews commented.

'Keeps the bodies fresher, you see,' Mr Waters croaked. 'They can smell bad enough already, without them decaying faster in the heat.' He gave out an unexpected chuckle, which caught the detective and Harvey by surprise. They had never heard him laugh before and were uncertain if this was his attempt at a joke. They smiled and nodded awkwardly in agreement, then, catching one another's expression, tried their hardest not to laugh out loud at the uncomfortable situation.

'So, you have something for me, I believe?' Matthews quickly changed the subject.

'Another report, I'm afraid, though I didn't think it should wait until Monday.' Mr Waters handed over a hand-typed report to the detective, who scanned it quickly.

'So this new death, it's a Mr Edward Welsh, nineteen years old,' Matthews read aloud. He quickly scanned the remaining document before speaking again. 'I don't follow.' He looked up at the coroner with confusion. 'This doesn't tell me very much at all.'

'Don't you understand, Detective?' said Waters. 'This report is almost identical to the one I gave you at the beginning of the week. It's almost word for word. He is a young man, with absolutely nothing wrong with him medically. He is in good physical health, and yet here he is dead.'

'And the autopsy again didn't show up anything?'

'Well, I did say the report was almost word for word. Mr Welsh didn't have an empty stomach like Mr Ainley, though this I predict to be because Mr Ainley had been vomiting a lot in the lead up to his death.'

'Did you find anything in the stomach suspicious?' Matthews looked back at the report in his hand.

'Well, there was a large amount of alcohol, but I don't think this killed him. I also found coca leaves. Quite a lot of them.'

'Would that be enough to kill him? Cocaine leaves are so widely available these days. Most people take it for ailments.'

'This is true. There was a lot in his system, though I'm not convinced there was enough to kill him.' Mr Waters continued, 'Coca leaves, unlike the other forms of cocaine, are usually taken to aid performance. I wonder if he was using them to help with his job.'

'Which was what?'

'When his body arrived yesterday, his mother came too. She spoke to me for a while and told me she was in shock because her son also worked with Bert Ainley, who, as we know, died last weekend.'

***

'Do you know where Mrs Welsh lives?' Harvey asked Matthews as they left the coroner's office thirty minutes later.

'Mr Waters has it written on the bottom of the report. He will have known I'd want it when he spoke to her.'

'And you think the coca leaves could be the cause?'

'Unlikely. But if Bert Ainley and Edward Welsh worked together, then there must be a connection.'

'But didn't you visit the building yard only the other day?'

'Yes, but Edward Welsh's name never came up, and there wasn't anything solid to pin them for Bert

Ainley.' Matthews lit a cigarette. 'Two deaths from the same building yard is enough to start a thoroughgoing inquiry.'

Matthews now marched back along the busy streets of Whitby. Despite the heat, the town was as busy as ever. They crossed the river via the swing bridge. Then walked up the steep street of Flowergate, passing Bert Ainley's bedsit on the left, and turned into a narrow road too slender for a horse and cart. Directly behind the grand, stone-built Crown Hotel on Silver Street was a three-story townhouse converted into three-floor apartments. On the ground floor was where Edward Welsh had lived with his parents. Matthews double-checked the address on the coroner's report before knocking. Mrs Welsh opened the door to them quicker than Matthews had anticipated.

'Ah, Detective.' She recognised him instantly, which was no longer unusual in Whitby. 'Please come in quickly before any of the neighbours see you.' She was in her mid-forties, wore a tired old floor-length green dress, and looked exhausted.

'Thank you, Mrs Welsh. I hope you don't mind my calling unexpectedly.' Matthews and Harvey entered her small sitting room, which also doubled up as a dining room, with a tiny wooden table and four chairs pushed up against the back wall.

'Tell ya the truth, Detective, I was expectin' ya.' She gestured for them to take a seat. 'Mr Waters had mentioned he would speak to ya, given Bert dying too.' She gave a quick sniffle, and it was clear she was trying to hold herself together. 'Would you like a drink?'

'No, thank you. We won't keep you long.' Matthews took out his pad and pencil just in case there was anything worth writing down. Harvey perched on the arm of the chair in which Matthews sat.

'My husband is in the kitchen. Do you need him too?' Mrs Welsh asked. Her voice was high-pitched for a woman her age. Matthews asked if Mr Welsh would join them, and after disappearing for a moment, Mrs Welsh returned with her husband, a round-faced man with greying dark hair and a rather large gut. Matthews thought he looked to be out of breath just walking from the kitchen.

"ow can we 'elp you, Detective?' Mr Welsh asked as he dropped himself into one of the other seats.

'I'm sure you can understand my wife is distraught at the moment, so I'd rather you didn't upset her longer than necessary.'

'I will keep this brief, Mr Welsh,' Matthews promised. Mrs Welsh perched on the arm of her husband's chair, mimicking Harvey's position.

'Tell me, had your son shown any signs of being unwell in the lead up to his death?' Matthews' use of the word 'death' set off Mrs Welsh into immediate sobs. She had clearly been trying to put on a brave face thus far.

'Now look what you've bloody done!' Mr Welsh yelled, pulling out a handkerchief from his trouser pockets and handing it to his wife.

'I... I'm so sorry, Detective.' She sniffed.

'The apology should be mine, Mrs Welsh.' Matthews was used to dealing with fragile people. He knew it best to give them time to talk, rather than having to come back another time, if at all possible.

'To answer your question, Detective...' Mr Welsh spoke with a tempered voice, '...no. He did not show any signs up until yesterday morning, and by the time evening had arrived, he had died.'

'Do you have any speculations about what could

have been the cause?' Matthews had a feeling Mr Welsh's patience would not hold out long, so he needed to get as much from him as possible and fast.

'I don't know,' Mr Welsh replied, a little more softly this time. 'It's come as a shock to us, that's for sure.'

'You're aware of a Mr Ainley, who has also died this week. I believe he and your son worked together?'

'That's right. In fact, he only lived on the next street, so we would often see Bert at ours, or our Edward would be around at his. Went to school together, you see. Known each other since they were little.'

'Did Edward ever mention anything about his job or the other people he worked with?'

'He would say things from time to time, but to be honest with you, Detective, I can't remember any of the other names he mentioned. It was only Bert who came around 'ere.'

'Have you ever seen Edward taking any kind of drugs?' Matthews asked, all the time hoping Mr Welsh didn't take offence at this.

'Not that I knew.' He looked at his wife, who also

shook her head. 'He went out a lot, often came back drunk. I told him he needed to get himself sorted and find somebody to settle down with, rather than getting drunk every couple of nights with his friends. Bert's death hit him hard. He came back every night this week worse for wear.'

'Other than work, was there anything else Edward did, anything you think I should know about?' Matthews could see this interview was not bringing up anything new at all. On his pad, he wrote simply that he needed to return to Edward and Bert's employer, and this time talk to some more of the other workers.

'Nah. We don't have the money to do things socially. Hanging around with Bert or going for drinks with his workmates is all he really did.'

'Well, don't forget...' Mrs Welsh interrupted, '...he enjoyed rowing too. He usually only did it once a week, but with the Regatta coming up, they were training most nights too...'

'Sorry.' Matthews stopped her. 'He rowed?'

'Yes. He joined the Whitby Friendship rowing team last year. They were supposed to be competing in the Regatta in about two weeks. Though I guess they will have to pull out now, with our Edward and Bert both gone.' Matthews and Harvey looked at one another, each one knowing exactly what the other was thinking. Both young men were part of the same rowing club. Perhaps this was the lead they'd been waiting for.

CHAPTER 7

SUNDAY 7TH AUGUST 1892

'Where on Earth did you find that?' the chief asked, picking up a miniature painting balanced on the fireplace.

'It's my grandmother,' Matthews replied, handing his father a drink. They had all returned from church, and this week, Grace and Matthews were hosting the family for dinner. Ever since Matthews and Grace had wed, they had taken it in turns to host the family meal. Last week had been at Matthews' father's house, and next week was due to be at Charlotte's home. The three houses were all within walking distance, which Matthews thought handy in some way, but a little too convenient in others. His father, who now lived alone since Charlotte moved out, often dropped in on one of his children unannounced. Thankfully for Matthews, Charlotte usually got these uninvited drop-ins, and she seemed not to mind as much.

'I know it's your grandmother,' the chief scoffed. His brash voice could be heard throughout the house. 'Bloody women lived in this same house, after all. Spitting image of your mother in this picture. Though where did it come from? I've never seen it before.'

'We found it in the attic a couple of months ago. She had a lot of things up there. Clearly collected from over the years, though why she decided to store this away is beyond me.'

'I wonder when it was made. She's awfully young in it. Must have been before your mother was born.' The chief inspected the image closely.

'Grace did actually take it out of the frame to give it a clean. The artist has signed it as 1824, and her name is Sarah Biffen. Though I'm not sure who she is.'

'Sarah Biffen was quite famous at the beginning of the century. I believe she toured the country, painting people. Biffen even painted Queen Victoria and other members of the royal family.'

'You seem to know a lot about her.'

'Well, she was famous. She didn't have any arms, you see, which is incredible to think when you look at the detail of this miniature. I, of course, am too young to remember her. She must have died when I was young. Though I've heard her name and seen some of her work. Fascinating to think your grandmother sat for her.' The chief returned the picture and took a seat in the living room, and at that moment, Charlotte's husband, John, joined the two men. Charlotte, who could barely move due to her belly's size, helped Grace in the kitchen, despite Grace pleading with her to put her feet up.

'She's ready to pop yet still won't sit down,' he told them both of his wife. 'I swear she is stubborn.'

'Just like her mother.' The chief laughed. 'Strong-willed women in this family. I did warn you before you married her.' The three of them laughed. 'I can't believe I'll be a grandfather again in a week. Now there's a title to make a man feel old.' His laughter roared. 'And at least this one I will get to see more of, unlike your brother, who never visits. That kid will be grown up before I see him again. Your mother would be furious if she was still around.'

'I don't think our Robert purposefully stays away.' Matthews tried to sound sincere. 'They'll come to visit if you ask them too.'

'Shouldn't need to bloody ask to see my own son and grandchild.' The chief took a seat in the living room and sipped his wine. 'Anyway, what's the situation with this new case of yours? One minute you're looking into something, next you close the case, now I hear it's back open. Second kid dead now, isn't there?' The chief couldn't help himself but talk work at any given opportunity. Matthews was surprised it had taken him this long.

'Now, now, boys,' Grace said, as she carried dishes through the sitting room to the large dining table at the back of the long room. 'No work talk over dinner we said.'

'We haven't started eating yet,' the chief protested.

'Well, I'm serving up, so please take a seat.' She disappeared again, and Matthews decided to follow her, knowing she would need help and that his sister shouldn't be doing any heavy lifting. He also wanted to get away from his father and the conversation of work.

'Come on, sis,' he ordered upon entering the galley kitchen. 'I'll help take these through. You go and take a seat.'

'Oh, you are a good brother and husband,' Charlotte mocked and squeezed past him, carrying a dish of potatoes. Her large belly made it difficult to fit between her brother and the counter. 'I think I can manage these.'

'You take these.' Grace handed over two dishes, though before he took them, he gave her a kiss. 'Come on.' She laughed. 'It'll go cold.'

'If I get to kiss my wife, then let it go cold.' And he took the dishes, placed them on the side, and pulled her in for a better kiss.

'Benjamin Matthews, control yourself. Your father is only in the next room, and he's waiting to be fed.' Grace couldn't hide her smile or her blushing cheeks. Matthews retook the dishes and pulled a silly face before leaving the kitchen.

'Is it just me or has this heat wave been going on forever?' the chief remarked as they all sat around the dinner table eating. 'Bring back winter if you ask me. It's too bloody hot, this.'

'I have to agree,' Charlotte replied. 'It's bad enough in the heat normally, but with this belly too, I can't move an inch without being exhausted and overheated.'

'That's why you need to take it easy,' Jo said, though she shrugged off his comments.

While Grace and Charlotte engaged in baby talk, the chief tried to sneakily talk work with Matthews. 'So, you mentioned there's a new lead?' He tried to whisper, though even this was louder than any average person whispering.

'Yes,' Matthews murmured. 'Bert and Edward were both a part of the Friendship Rowing Club. Harvey is looking into where they're based and seeing if the manager will speak to me. In the meantime, I'll be returning to the building yard. I need to speak to the foreman again now two of his men have died, and I want to see if I can speak to some of the other workers.'

'Good, good…'

'You're talking work again.' Charlotte jumped in, a grin on her face.

'Oh… erm… yes, well…' the chief stuttered. 'Will you be attending the Regatta this year? Only a couple of weeks away now.' His expression was proud for changing the subject so quickly.

'Well, I'll obviously have a new-born, so I'll have to see how we're getting on. What about you, Grace? Will you and Benji be going?'

'Oh, I imagine so.' Grace looked over at Matthews to see if he agreed. 'It's the biggest event in town, so we'll no doubt pop down to it at some point over the weekend.'

'The fireworks are always the best part, anyway,' Charlotte commented.

'You'll be pleased to no longer be heavily pregnant in this heat.'

'Oh, certainly. Though I hope for all our sakes this heatwave has gone by then.'

'Here, here.' The chief cheered.

Dinner was finally over, and after a couple of hours of drinking and socialising, it was time for everyone to leave. Matthews and Grace wished Charlotte well for her upcoming labour. They knew the next time they saw her would probably be with their new niece or nephew. Matthews still found it amusing that his baby sister was married and about to become a mother. He could still picture her as a young child playing with dolls and also getting dirty and playing rough with him and his friends on the beach.

'One last thing before I leave.' The chief cornered Matthews. 'The Friendship Rowing Club was due to partake in the annual boat race at the Regatta. I'm sure you've already thought of it, but make sure you find out who the other members of the team are; they might know more than the manager.'

'Yes, Pops. I'm hoping the manager will give me their details so I can question them too. Here's hoping they work at the building yard too, save me some legwork.' He tittered.

'Let's hope you get to them first,' the Chief said under his breath while placing his hat upon his head.

'What's that supposed to mean?' Matthews returned in a hushed voice, so none of the others, who were headed for the door, could hear.

'You can't tell me that two team members die weeks before the big race, and it's a coincidence.'

Matthews stopped for a moment to take in what his father was insinuating. 'I can't prove that yet. I can't jump to conclusions.'

'Maybe not,' the chief replied as he made for the

door, 'but if I was you, I'd be getting on with this investigation as quickly as possible. You could be on more of a time frame than you initially thought.'

CHAPTER 8

MONDAY 8TH AUGUST 1892

'Please stay home today and rest. You're clearly exhausted,' Matthews pleaded.

'I'll be okay. The fresh air and getting out of the house is just what I need. Stop worrying.' Grace sat at her dressing table and finished putting on her make-up as she spoke to her husband. She had had terrible morning sickness throughout the night and looked drained as she concealed the dark circles under her eyes. Although Matthews was right, she was determined not to let this pregnancy reduce her to a grievance or mollycoddling.

'I'm sure they'll understand. You need your rest.'

'What about your rest?' she protested. 'You were up with me all night too. You can't tell me you're not exhausted.'

Matthews didn't reply to her. It was true; he was beyond tired, but knew he had to get on with the case.

'Fine.' He finally surrendered. 'But I'll be taking you to work before I leave.'

'I can walk myself.'

'I have the carriage this morning. I'm going to see Mr Talbot again before heading to the office.'

'Who's he again?'

'The employer of Bert Ainley and Edward Welsh.'

'Ah, yes.' Grace stood, took a final look at herself in the mirror, and followed her husband downstairs. 'What time is Harvey due with the carriage?'

'He's just pulling up now,' Matthews replied, seeing the carriage through the sitting room window. He collected his satchel from the dinner table and escorted Grace out of the front door.

'Mornin', Detective.' Harvey was always cheerful, even at this time of the morning, though the heat was clearly getting to him too, as he looked drained.

'Harvey, we'll be dropping Mrs Matthews off at work on route to seeing Mr Talbot this morning.'

Matthews guided Grace to the carriage and opened the door for her.

'Right you are, detective. Mornin', ma'am.' He tipped his hat to her.

'Good morning, dear.' Grace had always liked Harvey, and he was often a regular visitor of the house. A polite young man, she was more than happy for him to call.

'Do you think it's time you quit your job now?' Matthews spoke softly in the back of the carriage to avoid Harvey hearing them.

'Why on earth would I do that? I enjoy my job, and you knew I didn't want to be just another housewife after we got married.'

'I know, I know, but I worry about you.' Matthews held her hand. 'This pregnancy is already taking its toll, and you're not even halfway there yet.'

'I appreciate you looking out for me, but I'd rather continue at the shop. Once the baby arrives, I'll take some time, but you know I already wish to continue for a couple of days a week afterwards. Joan has no issues with me bringing the baby in with me.'

'I know.' Matthews struggled to hide his disappointment. He was not upset with her for wishing to work, merely concerned about her and the baby.

'Plus, I have to help Beth make her wedding dress. That will keep me occupied. The last thing I want is to sit in the house thinking about being unwell.'

The carriage pulled up outside the dress shop on St Ann's Staith, just a couple of hundred yards from the Whitby swing bridge. The window display was of a mannequin wearing the latest fashionable, a floor-length pastel yellow with a matching hat. The wooden sign above the window, which was flaking and painted red and black, read: Popplewells - Fine ladies' attire. Est 1851.

'I will see you tonight.' She kissed her husband and exited the carriage.

"ave a great day, Mrs Matthews,' Harvey called after her. She gave him a wave and returned the gesture. 'To Mr Talbot now, sir?' he called back to Matthews, who was still sitting in the cab, leaning out of the window, watching his wife walk into the shop.

'Yes.' He sighed and watched Grace through the shop window as they pulled away.

It was mid-morning when they arrived at Mr Talbot's office on the edge of town, at Whitehall

Dockyard. Mr Talbot's labouring company took up a small area within the yard; the rest was primarily used for repairing cargo ships. Harvey decided to stay with the horses, leaving Matthews to speak to the owner on his own.

Upon arriving at the office door, Mr Talbot immediately looked displeased to see the detective. This was the second visit from him within a week, and he'd hoped not to have been disturbed again. Mr Talbot was a short man in his late fifties. He was already completely bald, yet with extremely bushy eyebrows and a pair of round spectacles balanced on his bright red nose.

'I already told you I don't know anything.' He spoke through gritted teeth.

'I assume you've heard about Mr Welsh?' Matthews asked, entering the small office and taking a seat without being offered.

'Of course I've fucking heard. Another bloody man down now. We have enough work piling up as it is. So excuse me, Detective, but I have little time to be fucking around with you and your ego today.'

'Mr Talbot, forgive me, but within a matter of days, you've had two employees die in suspicious circumstances. I recognise this is an inconvenience for you, but be aware that, at present, this puts you and your yard workers at the top of my suspects list. So you can either talk to me now for ten minutes, or we can do this at the station?'

'Fine,' Talbot replied, his face seething with fury with his reddened cheeks, tight clenched jaw, and furrowed brow. He threw his pencil down onto the desk and folded his arms like a child that had been told off. 'Now, what you wanna know?'

'You told me last time you didn't really remember Mr Ainley, but what about Edward Welsh?'

'A little bit.' Talbot's voice was sulky. 'We have quite a lot of men here; it's hard to remember them all. I don't socialise with any of them, so unless they're in trouble and I have to shout at them, I rarely spend time with individuals.'

'Do you know who Mr Ainley or Mr Welsh socialised with outside work?'

'Damned if I know!' Talbot was getting annoyed already. 'Look, Detective, I couldn't give a shit who they engaged with in their own time, as long as they turn up and do the fucking work. A couple of the lads are in the yard loading a cart with equipment.' He pointed out of the window and across the yard. 'Feel free to ask if they know anything.'

'Thank you. I think I will.' Matthews exited the office and strode across the yard as quickly as possible to catch the men before they left. There were young men, around late teens and early twenties, loading wooden beams onto the cart.

'Excuse me, gentlemen, could I have a word?'

The two men froze upon seeing Matthews. Like most people in the town, they knew who he was, and after hearing about their colleague's death, they knew why he was here. Matthews was used to people acting guilty before he had even spoken to them. He found that particular aspect of his job rather amusing.

'Of course, Detective,' the first man replied, dropping the plank of wood to the floor. Despite still being early, he was already covered in dirt as though he had already done a full day's work.

'Did either of you know Edward Welsh or Bert Ainley?'

'Sure did. Worked with both o' them for about a year now. Was sad and unexpected to hear they both died.'

'Do you know anything about what happened to

them? Or can you tell me when you last saw them?'

'It was a bit of a shock to tell the truth. I was out drinking with them both just the other week; it was a Wednesday, I think.' The young man turned to his friend, who nodded in agreement. 'Didn't see Bert after that. He was off sick the rest of the week, and we heard a couple o' days later he'd died.'

'Was it just a normal drinking session that night? Nothing more?'

'What d'you mean, Detective?'

'Did you see Bert or Edward taking anything? Drugs of some kind?'

'Well, they were both drinking that Vin Mariani.'

'What on Earth is that?' Matthews asked, confused.

'You know, the wine is made with tinctures of cocaine leaves. They used to chew the leaves a lot too. They were always talking about building up their muscle and performance in preparation for some boat race.'

'But coca leaves wouldn't kill them?' said Matthew aloud, unintentionally making it sound like a question.

'Nah, probably not. Though they did knock them

back that night, probably pissed and high in one go. I wouldn't be surprised if they were taking other things too. They were so focused on the race and winning. They hardly talked about anything else.'

'Do you know who else is part of their team?'

'I've never met them.' He again looked at his friend, who shook his head. 'We rarely spent time with them out of work. They came to the pub that Wednesday because it was James' birthday,' he gestured to the guy standing beside him. 'But other than that, they didn't usually spend time with us.'

'You mentioned you wouldn't be surprised if they were taking other forms of drugs,' Matthews said. 'Was anything ever taken or handed around here?'

The two men looked at one another before they answered. Matthews knew this look to usually mean people were debating whether or not to tell the truth.

'Hell no. The boss doesn't take well to things like that. A guy got fired once for injecting himself on the job. They say the foreman has a record, so he tries to keep his nose clean these days. Probably another reason he doesn't associate with his workers where possible.'

'Did either Bert or Edward look to be unwell in

the lead up to their deaths?'

'Bert complained about aches and pains a lot in the last couple of weeks, but to be fair, that's probably the laborious job and the rowing practise. He was fatigued a lot too. He got extremely drunk that night. We just presumed he was hungover when he didn't turn up to work the next day. Edward did turn up to work, but he was rough. He appeared to have a constant hangover for days and was distraught when we got the news about Bert. Seemed to hit him hard. I heard they were like brothers and went to school together, so hardly surprising, I guess. Ed was at work on that Friday he died, but he looked pale and weak. The boss shouted at him and accused him of being hungover again, so he sent him home. It was the next day we heard he'd died.'

Matthews thanked the two men for their time, asked them to contact him at the station if they remembered anything more, and returned to Harvey, who was still waiting by the horses and carriage.

'Anything?' Harvey asked as Matthews climbed into the cab.

'Interestingly, yes. Once you've dropped me off at the station, you can continue seeking out the rowing club manager and arranging a meeting for us. I need to hear what he has to say about two of his team dying.'

'Ya think he might be responsible?'

'Hard to say at this point. It's unlikely he'd want them dead when they were training to win.'

'Then don't ya have any suspects yet?' Harvey asked, concerned.

'Oh, I do indeed, but I need more evidence before I can prove it.'

Chapter 9

Harvey had successfully located the manager of the Whitby Friendship Rowing Club and had secured a meeting with Detective Matthews for this afternoon. Wishing to inspect the premises, the meeting had been arranged at the club. Matthews had been surprised to learn its location, down one of the narrow passageways, just off Church Street. Having never been interested in the sport before, he'd barely given a second thought about where the club was located before now.

'I'm afraid I can't go any further, Detective,' Harvey called back from the front of the carriage. He pulled the horses into the side and waited for further instructions. Matthews emerged onto Church Street, which was busy as usual. The cooler temperature brought a more upbeat atmosphere throughout the town.

'Stay with the carriage,' Matthews ordered. 'I'll meet you back here.' With that, he made his way up along Church Street and down the narrow alley towards the rowing club. Matthews had never been down there before, mainly because the passage only led to the River Esk's embankment. The opposite side of the river was filled with fishing boats and loading bays, a hive of activity throughout the day. However, this side of the river was completely different and had buildings built up to the edge, so nothing moored there.

The final building, before the river's edge, on his right-hand side, had a large wooden door, with the words 'Whitby's Friendship Rowing Club' written on it. He gave it a knock, and while waiting, peered his head around the corner of the building to see a large jetty with huge stable-like doors leading to it.

'You that detective?' A man's gruff voice came from behind him. Matthews had not heard the man open the main door and was startled by the sudden voice.

'Yes.' He cleared his throat. 'Are you Mr Singleton?'

'That's me. Thomas Singleton. Come in then.' Mr Singleton was nothing like Matthews had expected. He was tall, broad, and to Matthews, looked like he should be a lumberjack. He had an extensive shaggy ginger beard, red hair that was slicked back, enormous hands and arms covered in freckles, and a crooked nose as though it had been broken. A strangely good-looking man, in a rugged kind of way. He wore large, heavy boots, dark trousers, and a long-sleeved shirt that was open slightly at the top.

Matthews followed Mr Singleton into the building; it was more like a barn inside. There was a large rowing boat in the middle, which was more extensive than Matthews had expected. It was painted white on the external wood and had four seats for rowers and a smaller seat at the back for the fifth team member to work the rudder. The barn-like building had all kinds of equipment littered around the floor, from ropes to life jackets. There were oars hung on the wall and a shelf with trophies dating back years. Matthews was surprised by the lack of organisation the place seemed to be in, with the floor littered and the trophies coated in a layer of dust. It was clear to the detective that the team was less than bothered when it came to clearing away after themselves.

'Mr Singleton, I believe you know why I'm here?'

'Yes, and before you start accusing me of anything, I hope you've been looking into that bastard over at the Jet Works Rowers,' Mr Singleton spat. His voice echoed through the high ceiling.

'I'm sorry, who?' Matthews quickly searched through his satchel for his pencil and pad.

'Eric Herdman. He manages the Whitby Jet Works Rowing Club. He'll do anything to win the boat race, but this time he's gone too far!' His voice was deep and husky.

'Do you have any proof of this?' Matthews scribbled notes as they spoke.

'Of course not, but who else is it going to be? The Scarborough team wouldn't come all this way to do it, and Eric has been spying on our training sessions. He's seen we've improved this year. He'll do anything to win, that no-good rat.'

'Mr Waters, the coroner, found traces of coca

leaves in Mr Welsh's stomach. Did you know they were taking those?'

'Of course. I did. I told them to. It's well known that athletes use them to improve performance; it's not just rowers who do it either.'

'I see,' Matthews said as he jotted this down.

'A bit of leaf ain't going to kill 'em though, is it. The other teams have been taking it for years too, and none of them have died.'

'Mr Singleton, do you know if your team had been taking anything else?'

'No. It was Eric, I tell you. Probably slipped something into their drinks or something. I heard Bert was ill after he went out drinking. Well, that's probably it then, isn't it? Eric was probably at the bar looking to poison them. Have you checked with the pub? Did they see him there that night? I bet they did. The conniving pig.'

'I will make enquiries at the bar, though I have spoken to some of the young men they were with, and none of them saw anything out of the ordinary.'

'Well, they wouldn't, would they? How often do you go out for a drink and keep an eye out for somebody trying to kill you or your friends?'

Matthews hated to admit it, but Singleton had a point.
'You need to be asking the barmaid or the landlord;
they'll be the ones who know if he was there or not.'

'I would like to speak with the rest of your team if
I may.'

'Well, after Bert died, we postponed training until
we could find a replacement, then Edward died. I told
the rest of them we'd be lucky to find replacement
men at this late stage, but training would continue if
I found anybody. I haven't actually seen the others
since the day after Ed died.'

'Could I get their names and where they live?'

'Robert Clark and Peter Ward are the other two
rowers, then we have Billy Forster, the cox.'

'The what?' Matthews questioned.

'The coxswain. You know, the one who steers the
boat and keeps the rowers in sequence.'

'I thought you would do that.'

'I'm the manager. The boat would hardly win a
race with my fucking weight in it.' Singleton made to
snigger but decided against it.

'Do you know where they live?'

'I know where Billy lives. It's up in Fishburn Park.
Though don't ask me which house. He used to be

down here most days, even when there wasn't any practice. Though even he's stayed away these last few days. He knows where the others live too. I'd usually pass on messages to them through Billy if needs be.'

'Fishburn Park?' Matthews asked as he wrote it down.

'Yeah, quite big houses up there. Lives with his grandmother, but as I say, I don't know which house. Just turned fourteen. Nice and light for being the cox.'

'And what about the other two rowers?'

'I'm not sure about the other two. I knew Bert and Edward lived up around Flowergate, but again, I wouldn't have known exactly which houses. Robert works up at the Abbey Farm. You know the one, up on the cliff next to the Abbey, but I don't think he lives there too. Peter lives on the other side of town. He's our newest member, only seventeen he is, though a good bit of upper body strength for rowing.'

'Thank you, Mr Singleton. I will look into contacting them, and I will also look into Eric Herdman.'

'You should. Scheming little toad he is. I swear he's the one behind this. I'd put money on it.'

Matthews had a quick look around the boathouse, though he uncovered nothing of significance. He then took Mr Singleton's details, should he need to speak with him again, and thanked him for his time before leaving. Back on Church Street, he found the carriage waiting where he'd left them, but there was no sign of Harvey. Matthews quickly glanced into the carriage to check he wasn't sitting inside. It was empty.

'Sorry, Detective.' Harvey came running along the street. 'I only left for a second.'

'You know how important it is to keep an eye on them.' Matthews was stern but fair. Harvey looked genuinely sorry, and Matthews thought he looked as though he'd been crying. 'Is everything okay?' he asked as Harvey leaned past him to open the carriage door.

'Yes, sir.' Harvey gasped for breath. 'It'll never happen again, I promise.' Matthews jumped into the carriage, and Harvey closed the door behind him. 'Get everything you needed?' Harvey asked through the carriage window.

'Yes, I have plenty to tell you, but first, let's get back to the station. I have some street names and areas to look up before we move onto who we'll talk to next.'

The carriage pulled away from the hustle and bustle of Church Street and crossed the swing bridge back over to the West Cliff side of town. Once at the station, Harvey joined Matthews to his office, both of whom gave a quick hello to Mrs Lloyd-Hughes, who was tapping away on her typewriter, all the while surrounded by cigarette smoke.

'D-detective...' She gasped before bursting into a fit of coughs.

'Not now,' Matthews called back to her. 'We're looking something up. I'll come and get any post from you in a moment.' Matthews pulled out a large paper map of the town and unfolded it across his desk.

'Mr Singleton told me that Robert Clark worked at the Abbey Farm, up on the East Cliff... which is of course here.' He pointed to the map to show Harvey. 'He said that Peter Ward lived on the other side of town, which could be anywhere on West Cliff, so we will need to find out more to pin him down. Then the cox, Billy Forster, lives in Fishburn Park.' Matthews scanned the map.

'There it is.' Harvey pointed on the map. 'It wouldn't take us long to get there in a carriage.'

'Looks like a lot of houses in that area though. We don't know the exact one.'

'Shall we split up, sir?' Harvey suggested eagerly. 'I could start asking around Fishburn Park, see if anybody recognises his name.'

'And I can head to Abbey Farm and make enquiries about Robert Clark.' Matthews started folding up the map again and made to leave. Mrs Lloyd-Hughes appeared in the doorway, blocking him from being able to escape.

'Can it wait?' Matthews asked in a hurry.

'F-from your f-father,' she croaked. 'S-sorry, I m-mean the chief.' Matthews hated being referred to as the chief's son in the office.

'What is it?' He tore open the letter and scanned the content, gasping out loud.

'What is it?' Harvey asked, keen to know.

'Charlotte has gone into labour.'

CHAPTER 10

THURSDAY 11TH AUGUST 1892

Matthews was in his bedroom getting dressed for the day ahead. He and Grace had been anxiously waiting for any news of Charlotte since yesterday, though, so far, none had come. Upon receiving the information, Matthews had headed straight to the hospital, where he met his father. After hours of waiting, Charlotte's husband, John, had told them to go home. Matthews agreed, though his father refused to budge until he knew his daughter and grandchild were all right.

'Do you have to leave so early?' Grace asked, sat up in their bed, watching her husband. 'I don't have to be at the shop for hours yet. We could stay in bed together a bit longer.'

Matthews strode over to the bed and gave his wife a kiss on the lips. She cheekily placed a hand on his bare torso as he did so.

'I'm afraid I do,' Matthews finally replied, reluctantly pulling away from her and putting on a fresh shirt. 'Farmhands usually start early. I need to make sure I get up there this morning to talk to Robert Clark. I've no idea what time he starts or will be leaving.'

'Will you let me know if you hear anything about Charlotte?' Grace yawned.

'Yes, though you could very well hear before I do.' With his waistcoat loosely on, he checked his pocket watch and laced up his shoes. There was a bang on the front door. Matthews leaned up to the window to see if he could see who it was.

'I thought you said Harvey wasn't meeting you this morning?' Grace yawned again.

'He's not supposed to be. He's busy trying to get an address for Billy Forster.' Matthews couldn't quite see who was standing by his front door from his bedroom window, and so he dashed from the bedroom and down the stairs. Upon opening the front door, even Grace, who had remained upstairs, could hear who it was.

'It's a boy!' boomed his father. 'Arrived at two o'clock this morning, the little scamp.' He walked into the hallway without being invited inside.

'How's Charlotte?' Matthews enquired.

'Fantastic.' His voice echoed up the stairs. 'Came straight from the hospital to tell you the news. Mother and baby are doing excellent. John is, of course, delighted to be a father... and good heavens, I'm now a grandfather again and you an uncle again. Hard to believe, isn't it?' He was beaming with delight, yet he was clearly exhausted after being at the hospital all night.

'Yes.' Matthews was too tired for this level of excitement. 'Have they chosen a name?'

'They're calling him, Hugo.' The chief huffed. 'What kind of fucking name is Hugo?'

'What's wrong with it?'

'Well, it's hardly traditional, and it's quite common to name your child after your own parents, like you a lot, for instance. Benjamin was my father, Charlotte, my grandmother. It's how we've always done it.' Matthews now realised that his father was more upset not to have the child named after him.

'No offence, old man, but Hugo is a much better name than David.'

'You cheeky swine. My grandfather's name, that was. A good man he was too.'

'I have no doubts. Oh, I remember now,' Matthews interjected. 'John mentioned his grandfather was called that. They were Scottish descendants, though I've no idea if it's a Scottish name.'

'I didn't know that. Never met the man. I knew it wasn't his father's name. Oh, are you leaving?' the chief finally noticed Matthews was dressed and ready for work.

'As a matter of fact, yes.' Matthews turned and grabbed his bag, which was hanging on a hat stand. 'I need to get up to Abbey Farm this morning before coming into the station. Then I need to locate Eric Herdman.'

'Eric?' the Chief repeated, 'what are you looking for Eric for?'

'You know him?'

'Well, not that well. His wife is one of the typists at the station. I can ask her if her husband would be willing to come in for a chat with you.'

'That'd be perfect, Pops. Anyway, I really am going to have to leave.'

'Excellent, son. I'll catch up with you later. I'm off to bed for a couple of hours before heading to the station myself.'

They left the house together, Matthews glancing back to see Grace waving him on his way from the upstairs bedroom window. At the end of the street, he and his father parted ways. Matthews headed for Abbey Farm, and the chief headed home.

The walk to Abbey farm took the detective twenty minutes. The town was a little quieter at this time of the morning, though mainly because the fishing boats had already left and had yet to return with their morning catch.

At the top of the one hundred and ninety-nine steps, Matthews stopped to light a cigarette while admiring the town from this vantage point. The town always felt calm from up there, with the vast North Sea out to his right, looking like an endless watery desert that stretched on forever. To his left, the rows and rows of chimneys stretched down to the harbourside, houses and buildings lining both sides of the River Esk and into the distance. The past year he'd been back living in Whitby had passed by so quickly. Despite his initial objections to returning, he had to admit to himself that he was the happiest he had felt in a long time.

He was thinking about his sister and new nephew and how much he was looking forward to meeting him. It got him thinking about his own children and what he would be like as a father. He knew Grace would be a wonderful mother; she was so warm and caring to everyone.

As he finished his cigarette, he made a quick detour into St Mary's graveyard to visit his mother's grave. It was rare he visited it anymore, mainly at Christmas and her birthday like the rest of the family. Though standing there alone this morning was more enjoyable to him than he'd anticipated. The peace and quiet was calming, and a warm sea breeze against his face felt comforting. Yet this moment of reconciliation was quickly spoiled by a pair of seagulls passing overhead, their ear piercing calls bringing Matthews back to the here and now.

Detective Matthews left the graveyard and walked along Abbey Lane towards the farm. The ruins of

Whitby Abbey to his right and passing an old stone cross on his left, the farm was already in sight. Originally built as the main farm for the abbey, it was now privately owned and had fields of produce stretching along the cliffside into the distance. Although not the only farm around Whitby, it was one of the oldest and was the closest to town.

'Hello!' Matthews called, walking into the yard and seeing several people passing from building to building. A woman caught his eye and came over to speak with him.

'Can I help you?' she asked. She must have been about seventy years old. Her dress was covered in dirt, as were her hands, and she was wearing large boots that had dried mud all over them. She had a worn, kind-looking face, which was flushed after all the work she had done that morning already.

'Yes, I'm looking for a Mr Robert Clark.'

'Ah, are you Detective Matthews? I recognise your face from the newspaper.'

'I am, ma'am.' He gave a slight tilt of his head.

'Well, I'm sorry you came all this way, Detective, but I'm afraid young Mr Clark isn't here.'

'Does he not work here?'

'Well, he did, but I'm afraid he hasn't shown up for about a week now.'

'Do you know why?'

'Not heard a peep from him. It's not like him not to turn up; he's usually one of our most reliable land boys.'

'Have you not enquired as to his whereabouts?'

'I'm afraid we haven't enough hands up here as it is, Detective. I don't have time to go searching for somebody. There's work to be done. Our helpers come and go all the time, you see. Some are polite and tell us they're leaving, others just leave without a word. It's not unusual here.'

'Do you know where I might find him? Do you have a home address for him?'

'I don't, but if he turns up, I'll tell him you've been looking for him.'

'I'm afraid my finding him is somewhat time-sensitive.'

'How so?' Her reaction turned more concerned.

'His life could be in danger, and if he hasn't been at work for a week, we could already be too late.'

'Goodness.' She suddenly looked horrified. Turning her back to the detective, she called over to the other farm helpers unloading a cart full of produce they had already harvested that morning. 'Do any of you know where young Robert can be found?' The five men of various ages all shook their heads. 'I'm sorry, Detective, I don't think anybody here knows where he lives. He used to just turn up, do the job, and leave once paid. He wasn't one for hanging around. I couldn't really tell you much about him, come to think of it. Rather shy and reserved, really. I'm sorry I couldn't be more helpful.' With that, she walked away, returning to help unload the cart.

Matthews made to leave. 'Fuck!'

CHAPTER 11

Matthews left the house exhausted yet again this morning after Grace had had another terrible night of sickness. He felt ashamed of himself for briefly thinking that if Grace was to suffer like this every time, he might not want more than one child. Though he had refrained from sharing this thought with Grace. Matthews knew she had always wanted a large family, and he just hoped that she would feel better soon.

He had managed to convince Grace to stay home today and rest. As he left, she collected a pad and pencil to begin working on Beth's wedding dress design. He had hoped she would have stayed in bed to rest some more but didn't want to push her. After all, staying home was better than nothing.

'Please take it easy today.' He kissed her goodbye.

'I will.' She softly smiled, her eyes sleepy. She already had sketches of the dress outlined on the paper and began working on the detail and pattern. Grace had always enjoyed working in fashion. Her designs, Matthews thought, showed how incredible an artist she was. They had a large painting in the living room of the Whitby cliffs and ruined abbey, painted by Grace.

Through the living room window, Matthews saw as Harvey pulled up outside with the horses and carriage. Matthews had been concerned they had miscommunicated about the morning arrangements, as Harvey had been running slightly late. Something he never did.

'G'morning, Detective,' his cheery voice called out. 'Where to first?'

'Morning, Harv,' Matthews replied, his enthusiasm not matching that of Harvey in his tired state. 'It's straight over to East Cliff this morning. I have a meeting with Eric Herdman.'

'Is that the Jet Works Rowing Club manager?'

'That's the one. I want to check him out.' Matthews climbed into the back of the cab. 'Then it's back to the station for me while you keep looking for Billy Forster. I then need to come up with a plan to find Robert Clark and Peter Ward.'

The carriage soon sped off towards the harbour. Matthews made some notes on his pad during the trip. He was already starting to form a picture of what had happened to the two young men, but he knew he needed a lot more evidence before he could make an arrest.

They arrived in Market Square, which was already busy with stallholders setting up for the day. There were also plenty of people purchasing goods. Market Square was always filled with a bustling crowd throughout the day, with streets of shops branching off and the square filled with stallholders selling fresh produce daily. Matthews had noticed a change in the town these last couple of weeks. With the hot weather, people seemed to be keen on getting their shopping done quickly before the heat of the day became unbearable. He didn't blame them; even in the shade, the heat was exhausting.

'Harv, take the horses and carriage back to the

station. I will walk back today.' He was conscious of how they looked to be struggling the other day, and collapsed horses were the last thing he needed.

'Right you are, Detective.' Harvey turned the horses around, leaving Matthews behind in the square. Matthews squeezed his way through the crowds towards the Shambles indoor market. Beside the building was a narrow passage leading to a small stone-built pier named Fish Pier. It was so short that at low tide, the River Esk came nowhere near it. At the top of the pier stood a large building with enormous double fronted doors and a sign above that read 'Jet Works Amateur Rowing Club'. Matthews gave the giant oak doors a hard bang with his first.

'I'm comin',' a voice from within hollered. 'Detective?' he asked, opening a smaller inlet door and eyeing up Matthews.

'Yes. Mr Herdman, is it?'

'Yes, yes. Come in.' He stood back and invited the detective inside. Like the Friendship Rowing Club, this too had a large wooden boat in the centre of the room, with oars and other random items scattered around the vast open space. It was certainly a lot tidier than the other club.

'You'll know why I asked to speak to you, I presume?' asked Matthews as he dropped his bag to his feet.

'Yes.' Herdman sighed. His tone indicated he was fed up with the topic already. 'Gossip like this gets around town faster than cholera.' Mr Herdman was a stern-looking man with black hair slicked to the side and a large black moustache that almost covered his lips. He was much younger than the other team manager, with Matthews predicting him to be around thirty years old. He was also somewhat slender and shorter than the other manager too. He wore a suit despite the heat, and looked, to Matthews, as though he had never been in a rowing boat in his life. He also spoke a lot posher than Matthews was expecting.

'Mr Herdman, do you know any of the Friendship rowing team personally?'

'Not really. I've seen them at various boat races and Regatta over the years. I know the manager by name, Mr Singleton, of course, but I couldn't honestly have named his lads before reading about them in the paper.'

'Mr Singleton seems to believe that his team getting sick is a result of somebody sabotaging their chances at the upcoming Regatta.'

'Well, don't step around it, Detective,' Herdman groaned, 'what you mean is he's accusing me.' Herdman rubbed his forehead. 'If he thinks that's the reason, then, of course, he'll blame me. Not only are we the closest to them geographically, but we are their only real competition.'

'Meaning?'

'Well, our two teams and the Scarborough team are the only ones who have ever won or come close to winning in years.' Herdman spoke arrogantly. 'And, no offence, but the Scarborough lot have never actually won a race yet, to my knowledge.'

'And I take it you are above cheating?'

'I've been into rowing since I was a child, Detective. My grandfather was Harry Clasper. You heard of him?' Matthews awkwardly shook his head. 'He was a champion racer up in Tyneside. All of his children and grandchildren have gone on to do some kind of rowing.'

'And you're a rower too?'

'Only for fun. I'm not tall enough or muscular enough to do it competitively. Though saying that, Grandpa was shorter and slimmer than the norm too.

I've always preferred managing and training the team.'

'Mr Herdman, how long have you been managing this team?'

'Last year I took over. We did the Whitby Regatta, Scarborough Regatta, and Tyneside Regatta last year. So far this year, it's just the Whitby one left to do.'

'Did the Friendship club attend these too?'

'Friendship doesn't do the Tyne Regatta, but they do the Scarborough one. It was about three or four weeks ago now.'

'I see.' Matthews scribbled into his pad. 'I wasn't aware you all competed in other towns. Did you see the Friendship team at all in Scarborough? What was the race like?'

'I saw Singleton on the pier. We barely talk, if I'm honest. Friendship came second, and Singleton makes it all so clear to everyone in earshot that he doesn't like them not winning. I'm surprised he had a team left the way he shouts at them. I understand he's incandescent, we all are, but he makes a scene. He's capricious, and you never know when he will fly off the handle again. It's an embarrassment to the sport if you ask me.'

'Mr Herdman, other than this, what do you do for a living?'

'I work at the W Hamond Whitby Jet Shop, on Church Street. It's how I managed to get involved with the rowing team. The old team manager is the owner of the shop. I used to assist him until the beginning of last year when he fully handed it over to me. He still checks in from time to time.'

'Do you or your team ever take any enhancements to improve your rowing?'

'Such as…?'

'Coca leaves, or anything stronger?'

'I've heard many athletes use coca leaves, but I can't say I've used them personally. My team has won more races than any of the other local teams, so unless we start falling behind them, I see no reason to use anything more. If you ask me, it's hard work and good leadership that makes the team win. Drugs are just a cheat's way of slacking on the real hard work.'

'Mr Herdman, do you have any reason to believe that any of your own team would sabotage the Friendship team?'

'No. They feel sorry for them, having to put up

with that manager. I don't see any reason they would do anything to cheat in order to win.'

Matthews continued to talk to Herdman while he searched the boathouse, under the careful watch of Herdman. Yet, as expected, this uncovered nothing of value. He thanked Herdman for his time and returned to the station, where he remained for the rest of the day.

With Harvey trying to track down Billy Forster in Fishburn Park, Matthews wrote a letter to Doctor Bennett, asking if he recognised the names Robert Clark and Peter Ward. As a doctor, he knew many people around town, and Matthews was hoping he would be able to use these connections to pinpoint the two men.

At six o'clock, he finally left the station. This evening he had arranged to meet his friend Jack for a drink, though as he walked to the pub, his exhaustion meant he already wished he could go home. Despite his time-sensitive case, he had promised Grace that tomorrow they could sleep in. He was desperate for it too.

Matthews arrived at The Golden Lion Inn, one of the narrowest pubs in Whitby, positioned at the bottom of Flowergate. The public house was always dimly lit, with a dark wooden bar and merely a handful of small round tables with petite stools that were often rocky and unstable. The bar was lined with taller stools which had the same worn fabric as the smaller stools, but these ones were held together with tape. The scent of beer was strong the moment he walked into the bar, and aside from an elderly gentleman drinking and smoking in the corner, the bar was empty. With Jack nowhere to be seen, he made his way to the bar to order them both a drink.

'Now then!' came Jack's loud voice, just as the two pints of beer were placed in front of Matthews on the bar. 'I timed that right, didn't I.' He laughed and quickly took a sip from the one closest to him.

'Let's sit in the corner out the way.' Matthews grabbed his pint and made for the small table in the corner.

'Oh, I nearly forgot,' Jack said as he placed his pint on the table. 'Your little assistant is outside. Asked me to tell you to pop out.'

'Harvey?'

'Ey, that's him.' Jack slurped more of his drink.

'I won't be a minute.' Matthews sighed, standing

back up and heading back to the door.

'Don't worry, I'll have yours if you don't come back.' Jack laughed, and his voice carried through the whole of the tiny pub.

'I'd better have the same amount when I get back,' Matthews joked. He knew Harvey wouldn't be there if it wasn't necessary but was secretly hoping it was just a quick update before he went home. He stuck his head around the door to find Harvey leaning up against the wall. 'Everything all right?' he asked, making Harvey jump.

'Detective.' Harvey was taken aback. 'I've good news, and not so good news.'

'Better start with the good news.'

'I've found the Friendship club cox, Billy Forster. He lives in Fishburn Park as we were told. I 'ave his address, and he's 'appy for ya to go 'round there tomorrow to talk to 'im.'

'Fantastic.' Matthews beamed, taking the tatty piece of paper with the address on it. 'And the bad news?' Matthews braced himself.

'I also found where Robert Clark lives. You know, the one who worked at Abbey Farm?'

'Why is that bad news?'

'I was too late. He died this morning.' Harvey said with hesitancy.

'Ahh!' roared Matthews, his shriek echoing back into the pub through the still half-opened door.

Chapter 12

'What time is it?' Grace stirred, awaking to the sound of her husband trying to sneak out of the bedroom.

'A little after six o'clock,' he whispered back, then instantly wondered why he bothered whispering when she was already awake.

'I thought we were both going to have a sleep in this morning?' She began to sit up in bed. 'We've both been exhausted of late. Surely a little more sleep will benefit?'

'I'm sorry, I wanted to…' He yawned. 'It's going to be a long day, and I need to speak with the remaining members of the team before there are any more deaths.' He kissed her and left her to sleep. Matthews hurried on downstairs, collected his satchel, and made for the station. Standing on the doorstep as he locked his front door, he could see out over the North Sea, and the sun was just sitting above the horizon. The early morning sea breeze felt pleasant and refreshing, and he savoured every second of it as he walked along the street.

Arriving at the station, the place was eerily quiet. A couple of night officers were sitting in the small office beside reception. Other than that, the entire building was empty. Despite the sun now rising, his office was still dimly lit. Under the light of candles, which he lit and placed around the room, Matthews took out his notepad, spread the large town map across his desk, and began planning his next move to solve the case.

He was due to visit Billy Forster in a couple of hours, and he knew he would need to speak to the coroner about the latest victim, Robert Clark. His letter to Doctor Bennett should have reached the doctor by now too. But Matthews feared he didn't have enough time to wait on his response, so would personally have to visit him to see whether he knew of these boys' names, or at least the remaining one.

'Detective!' came the voice of Harvey from the doorway, startling Matthews. 'I saw yer candle on up here. I was about to get the horses ready to come and collect ya.' Matthews had already been there around an hour by now and was surrounded by scribbled notes. 'I also have something for ya.' He handed Matthews an envelope.

'What is it?' Matthews asked, trying to tidy up his now littered desk.

'I took the liberty of coming 'ere via Mr Waters' office to see if he had any information for ya. Thought it might save ya a trip.'

'Thank you.' Matthews eyeballed the envelope and ripped it open immediately. He instantly recognised the coroner's untidy handwriting. 'Well, just as I'd expect.' He handed the letter over to Harvey to read and slumped back in his chair. 'Similar findings, and he is certain of the use of some kind of toxin in the blood but can't identify it conclusively.' After a minute, when Harvey finished reading the letter, Matthews rose to his feet. 'Let's go,' Matthews announced, pulling on his bag and steering Harvey towards the door before he could utter another word.

'Where are we goin'?' asked Harvey.

'You're taking me to meet Billy Forster, and then we need to speak with Doctor Bennett.'

Half an hour later, Harvey was guiding the horses and carriage along Raglan Terrace, a small narrow street with terraced cottages lining one side and the small rear yards adjacent belonging to the terraced cottages on the next street. It was a quiet neighbourhood, which mainly consisted of houses. There was a pub and a paper shop around the corner, but other than that, you had to venture into the town centre for anything more.

'Here we are, sir,' Harvey called out to Matthews, who did not wait for Harvey to open the carriage door.

'Which house?' asked Matthews as he exited the carriage. They all looked the same at this point.

'That one.' Harvey pointed to the door closest to the detective.

'Tie the horses to the lamppost; you'll be able to keep an eye on them from the window.' Matthews knocked on the door as Harvey did this, and it was thrust open immediately. Clearly, the occupant had been watching out for them.

'Morning, Detective.' A scrawny young lad answered. He then looked over Matthews' shoulder and smiled at Harvey in recognition. 'Do come in.' He gestured them into the front sitting room. Harvey immediately stood by the window, and Matthews took one of the empty seats the young lad was offering.

'Mr Billy Forster, I presume?' Matthews rummaged in his bag for the notepad. 'The cox for Whitby Friendship Amateur Rowing Club?'

'Ey, that be me,' He was much smaller and younger-looking than Matthews had anticipated.

'Do you live here alone?'

'Nah, me gran's upstairs. Said she'd give us privacy, but if you want to speak to her too…'

'That shouldn't be necessary,' Matthews interrupted, 'but I will keep it in mind.' Billy took the empty armchair opposite Matthews and waited for what he expected to be some kind of cross-examination. 'Mr Forster, how long have you been the cox for the club?'

'Two seasons, sir.' He fidgeted in his seat. 'I was fourteen when I joined. There was a poster advertising it down by the docks, so I thought I'd give it a go. Mr Singleton was looking for someone small, less weight on the boat, I guess. Seems the only thing being short and skinny has been any good for.' He smiled as though trying to be humorous, though Matthews could see this was not humorous to him deep down.

'When was the last time you saw Bert Ainley?'

'We normally meet up for practice on weekends and one evening in the week. We were supposed to be practising on that Saturday, the day before Bert died, but none of the others turned up, only me. Mr Singleton was furious with them, said he would give them a right telling off. The last time we all practised was on Tuesday evening, five days before Bert died. We would normally do a Wednesday, but Bert and Edward had a work thing on Wednesday evening. Everyone else was more than okay to change days.'

'How did the four rowers all seem on that Tuesday?'

'No different than normal. They usually arrive before me to set up the boat and do some warm-up exercises in the barn before getting onto the water. Mr Singleton was going on and on about the Whitby

Regatta coming up and how we needed to up our game. He pushes the team hard, but then he says that's how we'll get better.'

'Are you aware of the four rowers taking anything to help their performance?'

'Erm...' Billy hesitated.

'I know about the coca leaves,' Matthews added.

'Ah, right.' Billy relaxed immediately. 'I knew they had those. Bert often talked about some beer, or something, that also had coca leaves in too, but I don't know if he had it often.'

'Did you never take anything? Coca leaves, or anything else?'

'No need, I only steer the boat and shout to keep the pace. Nothing too strenuous, really. Though Singleton does keep reminding me not to put on any unnecessary weight. We need to keep the boat as light as possible.'

'Had you ever seen the four rowers taking anything more than coca leaves or talking about anything stronger?'

'They were always pretty hush about that kind of thing. I didn't even know they were doing coca leaves for a long time. So it's unlikely they would ever tell me.'

'Mr Singleton is under the impression that Mr Herdman, of Whitby Jet Club, is sabotaging the team. What do you think of that?'

'I can see why he would think that.'

'Can you tell me why?'

'Two reasons come to mind. Mr Singleton is quick to blame anybody for anything he isn't happy about. If we lose, it's not him as a manager who's to blame. It's the team, weather conditions, and old equipment... always something. So blaming Herdman is not surprising, especially given they are our closest competitors. My other reason is that Mr Herdman is a bit of a snake.'

'In what way?'

'He acts all nice to people in public or at events when he's on show. He likes to tell people he is related to a well-known rower, manages to get that into conversation wherever he is. Everything is about appearance with him. But behind closed doors, I've heard he's not very nice. He has been known to hit his team if they don't do well enough, and he has turned up to events drunk on more than one occasion. Then, of course, he did threaten the

Scarborough manager, which I presume you will have heard about.'

'No. When was this?' Matthews asked while scribbling.

'At last year's Whitby Regatta.'

'Do you know what was said, and how do you know this?'

'They didn't realise I was in earshot. I was sitting down, changing into my wet shoes. The Scarborough rowing team manager told Mr Herdman that his team had been training night and day, and they were going to beat his team eventually. Mr Herdman, who was drunk at the time, told him that if their team beat his in their hometown, he would see to it that they never rowed again.'

'Did you tell anybody this?'

'I told our manager, Mr Singleton, at the time, though he shrugged and called it "competitive repartee". I didn't think much of it after that.'

'I'm still trying to track down the fourth rower, Peter Ward. Do you know where he lives?'

'Oh, yes. He lives just off Flowergate too. I'm not sure of the street name, but I could take you.'

'Certainly. Are you able to accompany us now?'

Matthews began stuffing his things back inside his bag before Billy had even answered.

'Sure thing. Let me just go upstairs and tell my gran where I'm going.'

Five minutes later, Matthews was in the back of the carriage with Billy Forster. Harvey had been instructed to head for Flowergate, and from there, Billy would direct.

'I take it you've heard Mr Singleton has posters up looking for new rowers already?' Billy asked the detective. 'He seems determined to still enter the Regatta.'

'I had not heard. When did these posters go up?' Matthews rolled his eyes.

'Yesterday,' Billy answered, all the time watching the view from the carriage window. 'I spoke to him yesterday. He told me to come back to training and be ready for the race.'

'Is there a forfeit if the team doesn't race?'

'No idea. Though knowing Singleton, he won't want Herdman to get the upper hand if it is 'im who done it.'

'Indeed.' Matthews breathed. It may seem insensitive, though he supposed the race would still be going on regardless.

'Detective,' Harvey called back to the cab sometime later. 'Doctor Bennett is walking just up ahead. He seems to be waving for me to stop.'

'Then do so,' Matthews called back. 'I had asked him if he knew the addresses of the rowers. It was a long shot, but he does know a lot of families in town. Though we don't need him now young Billy is taking us.'

'Doctor Bennett,' Matthews greeted through the cab window. 'I was planning on paying you a visit to follow up on my letter, but it turns out young Mr Forster here has the information I require.'

'That's what I flagged you down for, Detective.'

'Oh?' Matthews looked concerned.

'It's Peter Ward, whom I presume you are headed to right now.'

'Oh, shit. Don't say I'm too late for this one too.'

'Not yet, but he isn't at home. I've just had him sent to the hospital. If you're fast, you might catch him before he dies.'

Chapter 13

Saturday 13th August 1892

atthews ordered Harvey to turn the horses around immediately and instead head for the hospital. Billy Forster, who was still in the carriage, insisted on coming along. Matthews, who did not have time to argue this, agreed to it on the understanding that police business came first.

'Of course,' Billy replied, looking pale and in shock.

The ride to the hospital was short, and even before they had come to a complete stop, Matthews threw open the carriage door and ran towards the hospital entrance. A young nurse in her early twenties, with auburn hair and a flushed complexion, was filling in some paperwork at the reception desk when Matthews came running in.

'May I help you, Detective?' she asked, stopping what she was doing and approaching him. He was well known at the hospital, having requested to speak to many patients for various reasons over the past year.

'I would like to see Mr Peter Ward. Doctor Bennett informs me he was brought in today.' The nurse glanced at Harvey and Billy, who had just entered and now stood beside the detective.

'I'm afraid he's very unwell, Detective. His mother, is currently sitting with him, and he's not responding at the moment.'

'Then please may I speak to Mrs Ward?'

'I can take you to the room, and we can ask, though I warn you she is terribly upset.' She gestured for Matthews to follow. 'I will need to ask you two gentlemen to wait here,' she told Harvey and Billy.

'Harvey, would you mind waiting with the horses?' Matthews quickly asked before following the nurse. He then turned to Billy and wondered how to get rid of him too. 'Billy, I'll ask somebody to let you know once he's available for visitors.' Billy nodded and looked as though he would cry, but managed to keep himself together and followed Harvey back outside. Matthews then followed the nurse as she exited the reception and began walking towards a long corridor.

'Mr Ward was brought into us not that long ago, Detective,' the nurse informed him as she guided him along the hallway. 'The doctor has put him on a drip, and he will have samples of blood and urine taken shortly for testing.'

'Do you know what condition he was in when he arrived?'

'Unconscious, and still is. Apparently, he collapsed this morning at home. Mrs Ward called for the doctor, but Doctor Bennett immediately sent for an ambulance.'

'Do you have any idea what could have caused his sudden collapse?'

'It's too early to tell for sure, but he is showing typical signs of overdose.'

'Overdose of what?'

'That can sometimes be difficult to tell. Our tests will hopefully give us a better understanding.' She stopped outside a private room; a circular window in the door allowed the detective to see the motionless Peter Ward lying on the bed. An older woman sat beside him, holding his hand. 'Detective, Mr Ward needs rest right now. Once he wakes and is fit enough to speak with you, we can send for you.'

'Thank you.' Matthews smiled. 'I will just see if Mrs Ward is willing to speak with me before I leave.' The nurse bowed her head as she turned to leave.

Matthews gave a gentle knock on the door before letting himself in. Mrs Ward looked up and seemed surprised, as though she was expecting somebody else. The room was small, with bare walls and a small window that looked out onto a brick wall. There were two wooden chairs for visitors, one occupied by Mrs Ward, and a side table with a lamp perched on. The thick walls of the hospital made the room a lot cooler than outside.

'You're not the doctor,' Mrs Ward whispered. She had a rounded figure, and her dark curly hair looked windswept. She was wearing a light blue summer dress.

'No,' Matthews replied in an equally low voice. 'My name is Detective Matthews, and I was wondering if you'd be happy to speak with me for a moment.'

'What do you wanna know?' She sniffed, her tired eyes fixated on her pale, lifeless son.

'I just want to ask you some questions about your son and the Friendship Rowing Team. Would you be willing to step outside with me? There's a small room at the end of the corridor we can sit in privately.'

'I can't leave him.' She began to cry. Matthews handed her his handkerchief.

'I promise to not keep you long, Mrs Ward. Unless you'd rather we spoke here?'

'All right,' she said while rising to her feet, 'but not here. Let's go sit somewhere else.'

She walked around the bed, and Matthews held open the door for her. They made their way to a small waiting room at the end of the corridor, which was currently empty. It had a small frosted out window, five armchairs that were all worn and beginning to break, and a small open dormant fire. Matthews closed the door behind them for privacy.

'Doctor Bennett told me that someone from the station would likely wish to speak with me.' She huffed as she threw herself into one of the chairs. 'I didn't quite expect you to jump on it this quickly. I've only been in the room with him for a couple of minutes.' She rubbed her eyes, which were red and tired. 'Now, what can I help you with, Detective?' Mrs Ward spoke louder now they were alone.

'Your son is part of the Friendship Amateur Rowing Club?' Matthews refrained from taking out his notepad this time; he could sense Mrs Ward was not happy to be interviewed at that moment in time. Bringing out a pad may antagonise her further into fleeing back to her son. He would have to make sure he scribbled anything of importance down afterwards.

'He is, though why he ever joined is beyond me.'

'You didn't approve?'

'He should have been out there working and bring back money for us to live off, not wasting his time paddling in the water.'

'Did your son not also work?'

'Yes, but his father is out there working two jobs to keep our family fed. On the other hand, Peter wastes his time in boats instead of looking for anything else that could bring in some extra money.'

'Do they receive prize money if they win?'

'If, being the keyword there, Detective. I've told

him time and time again he's wasting good money-making time on it.'

'Mrs Ward, do you know the other rowers on his team, or the manager, Mr Singleton?'

'Not personally,' Mrs Ward scoffed, 'I've never actually met any of them, though Peter occasionally talked about them.'

'You never even met them at one of the races?'

'I don't have time for that nonsense, Detective. Some of us don't have the luxury of social time or fun.' She fidgeted in her seat, Matthews consciously trying to get as much out of her as quickly as possible.

'You say that Peter sometimes talked about them. Do you recall anything in particular?'

'No,' she scoffed, and Matthews was worried he was about to lose her. 'I don't think he likes the manager much, and as far as I'm aware, he doesn't hang around with the other rowers outside practice.'

'Are you aware of your son chewing coca leaves?'

'My Peter wouldn't even know what that was.' She looked at Matthews, offended by the suggestion. 'Cocaine, isn't it? Seems like most people are chewing it or smoking it these days. Not me, though. Filthy habit. Stick to regular cigarettes if you ask me. Much better for you.'

'Mrs Ward, your son is showing signs of a potential overdose. Can you think of anywhere he might have gotten something to do that?'

'I'm telling you, Detective, my son doesn't do that kind of thing, and if it was an overdose, then somebody else must have given it to him.'

'Can you think who?'

'Well, clearly those other rowers have been on it. They must have pressured my Peter into it. I told him to get some more work. No good comes from playing around in paddle boats with hooligans.'

'How do you know about...' Matthews started.

'The whole bleeding town has been talking about it. That's why I kept Peter away from them this week. Told him he wasn't allowed to row anymore.'

'And what did he say to that?'

'Well...' She hesitated. 'He wasn't happy, but I know in time he'll see I was right. I mean, look at him now. Clearly whoever harmed him is connected to the rowing clubs somehow. If you ask me, the lot of them should be shut down and told to get real jobs or be thrown in jail.'

'Mrs Ward, when Peter wakes, I would like to

speak to him.'

'If you must, but I'm telling you, you won't learn anything more. I know my Peter, and he would never get involved in that kind of thing. He has clearly been poisoned by somebody, and I won't rest until you catch the culprit. Now, if you don't mind, I wish to return to my son.' She stood and headed for the door. 'You have a murderer to catch. Good day.' She left the room quickly before Matthews could say anything further.

The detective was used to dealing with protective parents, and parents who wouldn't see their children as anything but innocent victims. Though Matthews did not see Peter Ward as a villain, he was undoubtedly not as squeaky clean as his mother would lead him to believe. Before leaving the waiting room, Matthews pulled out his notepad from his satchel and scribbled down as much as possible.

Ten minutes later, Matthews returned to the carriage. Harvey had been standing talking to the horses when Matthews had appeared.

'Did ya get to speak to 'im?' Harvey asked, seeing Matthews' expression looking less than hopeful.

'No, but hopefully soon.' He climbed into the

carriage and took out his notepad to read notes from the entire case. 'Harvey.'

Harvey stuck his head through the carriage door. 'Yes, sir.'

'I'm going to send you on a little assignment.'

'I need to stay local in order to see Mr Ward when he awakens. However, I also need to arrange a meeting with the Scarborough Rowing Club manager. Mr Herdman kindly gave me his details when I spoke with him, though I didn't at the time think they were necessary. I need you to get the train to Scarborough and arrange a meeting for me.'

'I've never been on a train before, sir.' Harvey looked rather excited.

'Let's get these horses back to the station. I'll see you onto the train with a letter for a Mr Basset.'

'Do you think Mr Basset will be useful?'

'I do, though it's Peter Ward waking up that is more imperative right now. I just hope he's strong enough to survive.'

CHAPTER 14

SUNDAY 14TH AUGUST 1892

'**C**ome now, or we'll be late for meeting our new nephew,' Grace called up the stairs. Matthews had been reluctant to attend the church service that morning due to being engrossed in his current case. He had argued how time-sensitive his investigation was and that church would have to wait until next week. He had been working late into the night, poring over his notes, trying to see if there was any possibility that he was overlooking something. So this morning, he was exhausted. Keen to get him away from his work, if only for a short time, Grace had managed to drag him reluctantly to the service. However, she had been made to promise they would return home straight afterwards. After over an hour back home, they were due to leave for Charlotte's house for dinner and finally meet her new son.

'I'm coming,' he called back to her, though in truth he was halfway through scribbling more questions, aimed primarily at himself. Harvey had managed to secure him an interview with Mr Basset, the Scarborough Rowing Club manager, tomorrow morning, so he wanted to be prepared for that. He was also still waiting for any news on Peter Ward's condition and hoped he would survive to testify.

After another ten minutes and further calls from Grace, Matthews finally appeared downstairs, ready to leave. Since having her baby, Charlotte had made the decision to attend a church closer to home instead of St Mary's at the top of the East Cliff. Their father had also decided to frequent the other church and spend time with his daughter and grandson. Matthews and Grace attended the regular church service. It was where they had been married, was the place his mother was buried, and because he saw this as the perfect excuse not to have to spend the entire day with his father. Though their relationship was much better than that of a year ago, they were still not the closest of family members.

'I wonder how Charlotte and John have been getting on,' said Grace as they left the house. Matthews shrugged. 'Well, I hope you're a little more enthusiastic when our baby arrives.'

'Oh, yes. Sure.' He felt a sliver of guilt. He'd been so caught up in his inquiries that he had barely spoken to Grace in days. 'I'm sorry.' He kissed her on the cheek before they started walking. 'It's this case.'

'Are you any closer to solving it?' She linked her arm with his as they walked along the road.

'Everybody I speak to has blamed somebody different, which isn't unusual, but...'

'But what?'

'Normally, you can get a good idea who's lying through their teeth or trying to cover up their own guilt. This case is different. All of them are acting guilty, yet they all seem convinced with who they're blaming.'

'Do you have many people left to speak to?' Grace asked, more concerned with her husband and how long this case would go on.

'I have a meeting with the Scarborough rowing

manager tomorrow, but it's Peter Ward I need to speak to the most. I just need him to wake up.'

'I'm sure he will.' Grace tried to sound sincere but knew her husband could see straight through her attempts at saying the right thing.

'Anyway, let's just enjoy this afternoon.' Matthews changed the subject. 'No more case talk for the rest of the day.'

Charlotte and her husband, John, lived only a short walk away from their own home. They turned right onto Crescent Avenue and walked around the vast Church of St Hilda's and onto Church Square. Charlotte and her husband lived in a prominent red-brick townhouse. The large church was the main view from all of their windows to the front, and their rear windows overlooked Royal Crescent and the North Sea beyond. They had moved into this house shortly after marrying. Since then, Charlotte had been enthusiastically redecorating all of the rooms bright and elaborate colours. Her eccentric taste was not typical of the rest of the family but was undoubtedly representative of her personality.

Knocking on the door, they were quickly welcomed inside by Matthews' father, whose deep voice called back into the house, announcing their arrival.

'Just in time, brother. Dinner is about to be served.' Charlotte pulled her brother in for a giant hug before giving Grace a gentler peck on the cheek.

'Would you like some help?' Grace was quick to volunteer. Charlotte gladly took her up on the offer, and the pair of them disappeared into the kitchen.

'Where's the baby then?' Matthews inquired, following his father into the sitting room and seeing John in there alone.

'Just got him down for a doze. Hopefully, he'll stay there while we eat and then he came come down and meet his Uncle Benji and Aunt Grace.' John beamed with delight, though Matthews could also see the exhaustion in his face. Without even being asked, John began telling Matthews everything about the baby, including nappy stories Matthews thought seemed inappropriate just before they were about to eat.

'You have it all to look forward to.' He slapped Matthews on the arm and laughed.

'Well, I know who to come to for advice.' Matthews gave an awkward smile, all the while wondering what was keeping Grace and Charlotte.

Dinner was more enjoyable than Matthews had anticipated. His father was more interested in talking to Charlotte and John about their new son than anything else, so it allowed him the afternoon free from work talk.

'Yes, well, he would make a fine officer one day. Already a powerful thing, he is. Those legs are already strong.' He announced. 'Though it will be his choice, of course.'

Matthews had to hold back a scoff. He had never had the luxury of being able to choose his own career. It seemed hypocritical to Matthews that he, having been pushed into this career, should now hear his father say his grandson could decide for himself.

'When will the christening be?' asked Grace.

'We're speaking with the vicar on Tuesday to arrange a service and the date.' Charlotte looked at her husband as she spoke, her face brimming with happiness. 'We're hoping sometime in the next couple of weeks. We were going to ask…' She stopped and looked more intently at John, as though willing him to continue.

'Oh, yes…' John choked on his food, taken a little

by surprise that Charlotte had chosen now for this. 'Charlotte and I were wondering if Grace and you…' he turned to address Matthews, '…would consider being godparents?'

Matthews, who couldn't help but wonder if meeting the baby before being asked would have been the correct order of events, was interrupted by Grace before he could answer.

'Of course we would!' she shrieked and immediately rose to her feet to embrace Charlotte. Matthews took her lead and shook John's hand.

'Be delighted to.' Matthews smiled. He hadn't even considered being asked.

After dinner and right on cue, noise from upstairs indicated that baby Hugo was awake. Charlotte excused herself to attend to him. John invited the rest of them back into the sitting room to await Hugo's arrival.

'So, is your final rower still alive?' The chief asked Matthews while they waited. He knew he wouldn't be able to avoid work conversations the entire evening.

'I haven't heard any updates today, so I assume the situation hasn't changed.' He sat next to his father on the sofa, deciding to go along with the work conversation and hoping this would get it over with sooner.

'Here's hoping he recovers; his testimony will likely be the only one you'll need.'

'Yes,' Matthews replied, somewhat sombre.

'I hear the rowing team has already been fully replaced now. Bunch of fishermen I believe he's recruited. Makes sense, I suppose. Already used to the open water and usually a strong bunch of men. He'll be hoping that will be enough to see them win.' The Chief bellowed.

'Do you not think Mr Singleton's lack of empathy is questionable?' John asked.

'I thought that the first time I heard he was recruiting.' Matthews replied.

'Just because he hired a new team doesn't mean he doesn't care,' the chief barked. 'Take me, for instance. If I lost half the squad, I'd be devastated, but I would still be looking to replace them as soon as possible.'

'Fair point,' Matthews replied. 'What's taking her so long?' He turned to ask John, desperate for Charlotte to return so the conversation could be switched.

'Probably changing him. She shouldn't be long.'

Nonetheless, John decided to check and headed upstairs.

'How's Harvey getting on with the training?' The chief turned back to Matthews.

'Oh, I think he looks so sweet in his new uniform,' Grace interjected.

'I believe he's enjoying me giving him more responsibility. When I don't have anything for him, some of the other senior officers take him along on patrols.' Matthews had undoubtedly come to appreciate Harvey over the past year and valued his assistance, especially in more prominent cases.

'I hear he's been acting a little odd these past few weeks?' The Chief commented, making it sound more like a question.

'Odd?' Matthews repeated. 'In what way?'

'Several of the senior officers have mentioned he seems less interested in the training than he did initially. As though he's more preoccupied and less focused on the job.'

'I can't say I've noticed.' Though Matthews realised he'd not spent that much time with Harvey during the past week, and the times they had been together had been brief. It was plausible that Harvey was acting differently and that he hadn't noticed. After all, he was focused on the case, not to mention a wife at home who spent most of the night being sick. Maybe he did need to pay a little more attention to other things, not just the investigation.

'Here he is!' Charlotte announced as she carried in her newborn baby. 'Let us meet your Uncle Benji first, shall we.' She handed over the baby to an unprepared Matthews.

'Oh… erm.' Matthews wasn't sure what he was doing and found himself more nervous about this than anything he had ever faced in his police career.

'Am I holding him right?'

'Of course.' Charlotte laughed. 'Just relax; you're doing fine.'

'Will be good to practise for when your own arrives,' the chief remarked, a gentler volume now in the presence of the baby.

'Well, I suppose hello.' Matthews looked down on his little nephew, whose wide prominent blue eyes were looking back to him.

'Do you think he looks more like me?' Charlotte asked her brother.

'Erm… I don't know. He just looks like a baby to

me.' Charlotte and Grace giggled at his comment, though his father and John nodded as though in agreement.

CHAPTER 15

Grace had had yet another bad night of sickness, and Matthews had tended to her throughout. He had been pleading with her to call the doctor, but she had refused him. She was adamant the doctor was not needed and that she simply needed to get through these first couple of months of pregnancy.

'My mother was terribly ill during her first two or three months,' she informed him, 'but after that, she was okay.'

'I hate seeing you like this.' Matthews held her. His arms wrapped around her as they laid in bed.

'It won't be for long.' She forced a smile. 'We will

forget all about these foul nights when the baby arrives.'

'I hope you're right.' Matthews knew it was unlikely he would ever forget this. The sound of his wife violently vomiting in the middle of the night was a sound he feared would never leave him. He wished beyond anything there was something he could do to make her well. They must have fallen back to sleep as Matthews stirred to find Grace no longer lying next to him.

'Grace!' he shouted from the bed, just as she walked back into the room.

'I'm okay.' She smiled. 'What time are you leaving this morning?' Grace asked, climbing back into bed. Matthews leant over to retrieve his pocket watch from the bedside table.

'Shit, Harvey should have been here by now.' Matthews jumped out of bed and peered out of the bedroom window. 'No sign of him yet. I'd best get dressed.' He had never slept in before and was usually up at the crack of dawn. These late nights comforting Grace had finally started to catch up with him.

'He's never normally late,' Grace commented as she tucked herself back in. 'In fact, it's usually the other way around. One can never sleep in when Harvey is due to arrive. He's always early.'

'Indeed.' Matthews buttoned up his shirt and peered through the window again. 'I better go. Perhaps something has delayed him. I have a meeting with Mr Jesse Basset today, so I'll need to get going.'

'Which one is he again?' Grace struggled to keep up with all the names.

'The Scarborough Rowing Club manager.'

'Ah yes, of course.' She yawned. 'The Regatta starts on Friday, so I'm sure he'll be anxious in anticipation of that anyhow.'

Matthews left the house a couple of minutes later. Harvey and the carriage were still nowhere to be seen. Matthews started walking in the direction Harvey would be travelling, just in case.

Matthews made it all the way to the station without seeing Harvey, and as he was about to walk through the station door, he heard someone calling him from the street.

'Detective,' came the out of breath voice. 'Detective... Matthews.' It was Harvey.

'Ah, there you are. I was beginning to worry.'

'I'm so sorry, Detective. It will never happen

again,' Harvey told him, between trying to catch his breath.

'Is everything all right?' Matthews was concerned. This was the first time Harvey had ever been late, and with what his father had told him yesterday, he was now even more apprehensive.

'Yes, sir.' Harvey straightened himself up and dusted off his trousers, which had collected a lot of dust in the run. 'It won't happen again. I simply lost track of time this morning when doing my chores. Do you need the horses ready?' He looked exhausted, but Matthews couldn't tell if it was down to his lack of breath or something more.

'Not this morning.' Matthews knew Harvey was intentionally changing the subject. 'We have the meeting with Mr Basset in a couple of hours, so we'll need to leave for the train station shortly. I will meet you back here in half an hour, and we can go together.'

'You want me to come?' Harvey beamed with delight; he loved being taken on investigation work.

'Of course. You set up the meeting; it's only right you attend it.'

Thirty minutes later, Harvey was waiting for the

detective outside the door, just as they had agreed. After being late that morning, he was determined to make sure nothing else went wrong for the remainder of the day. They walked to the train station and purchased tickets for the ten o'clock train. The platform was already busy with a throng of people coming and going. The noise of people talking loudly and the sound of luggage being moved and trolleys clattering along the stone floor all added to the mayhem. The train, which had recently pulled into the station, was throwing up a vast amount of steam.

A handwritten sign displayed the timetable of trains leaving the station today—the one leaving after the Scarborough train was bound for York. Matthews smirked to himself, amused at how different his life had become since arriving back from York over a year ago. How on that very same train ride he had met Grace for the first time, and how much he had resented coming back to Whitby. He wondered if he had returned to York, how his life would look now. Would he be happy? Or would he still be living in the tiny bedsit overlooking York Minster? Matthews knew he would always miss the cosmopolitan feel of the big city, and the way of life seemed to be much different. Still, he knew that in itself was no guarantee of happiness.

'Detective, we can board now.' Harvey nudged him, realising he was somewhere in his own head.

'Right.' Matthews led the way up the platform and boarded the nearest coach. It was clear that Harvey was excited about going on a train again. Matthews found them a pair of seats and allowed Harvey the one by the window for the journey. The route along the coast was beautiful, with rolling hills and farmland to the right and the North Sea occasionally coming into view on the left. Matthews realised this was his first ride on this route because the line was only opened six years ago.

Finally arriving at Scarborough station, an hour later, Harvey could see Mr Basset through the train window sitting on one of the station benches, waiting for them.

'That's him.' He elbowed Matthews and pointed at the man. He was smartly dressed, with a dark complexion and a thin moustache. A round bowler hat sat upon his head. Mr Jesse Basset had been looking out for them. Upon seeing Harvey peering out of the window, he gave him a wave of acknowledgement. The seafront was quite a walk from the station, and so Mr Basset had promised Harvey to speak with Matthews at the station for convenience. Though he had refused to come all the way to Whitby himself, especially when he was coming to town for the Regatta in a matter of days anyway.

'Mr Basset.' Matthews extended a hand as he approached the seated man. Basset rose to his feet and returned the handshake. Matthews was immediately stunned by the man's sheer size, being both muscular and taller than Matthews. Mr Basset gestured for the detective to take a seat on the bench beside him.

'So what can I help you with, Detective?' His voice was deep and his accent unrecognisable to Matthews.

'As I'm sure Harvey here has already informed you, I'm investigating the deaths of the Whitby Friendship Rowing Team.'

'Yes, he mentioned that bit.' Basset coughed and looked cautiously at members of the public who were still disembarking the train, clearly waiting for the platform to clear before continuing. 'Detective, I appreciate you coming all this way, but I will be in

Whitby on Friday for the start of the Regatta. Could this not have waited until then?'

'I'm hopeful that this will all be cleared up before then, if possible.' Matthews took out his notepad, but Mr Basset seemed uncomfortable at the sight of it. It was common that the sight of him taking notes made people more uncomfortable, as it was a sign the conversation was going from informal to formal.

'I don't know what you think I can do to help, Detective.' He spoke more openly now with the platform cleared of people. 'I don't go into Whitby except for the annual Regatta, so I surely wouldn't have any information of use for you.'

'Can you tell me a little bit about Mr Singleton, the Friendship Team's manager?'

'He is a fool,' Basset blurted out. 'I'm sure by now you've met the man, and you would agree. I wouldn't put it past him to clandestinely poison his own team just to try and pin the blame on somebody else. He's a sore loser; that team deserved better.'

'What about Mr Herdman, of the Jet Works Rowing Team?' asked Matthews.

'He's a psychopath too,' spat Basset. 'Thinks he's something extraordinary, just because he's a relation of Harry Clasper. All he does is eulogise Clasper and tries to build his reputation and stature off him. We all know Harry was a great man, but that doesn't mean Herdman is.'

'Do you think Herdman is capable of something like this?'

'Wouldn't put it past him either. The Friendship team was certainly improving. I would have even put money on them winning this upcoming Regatta, but that's more to piss Herdman off. Herdman hates losing, despite his team often winning. He certainly wouldn't take it well should the other team beat him in their hometown.'

'Are you aware of any medication or substances being taken by any of the rowing teams?'

'What athletes don't use stimulants these days.' Basset scoffed. 'Be it rowers, runners, or any of them, all on something to make them perform better.'

'What kinds of things?'

'Well, of course, tonics are the main source.' Basset lowered his voice again as passengers began to pass them again to board the train back to Whitby. 'All kinds available, though I suppose you know that. Hardly black market shit. Then there are cocaine leaves which are popular to chew, though to be honest, I never personally saw any benefit of those.'

'Any other things that can be used?'

'Many athletes inject strychnine or tinctures of cocaine, and of course, sips of alcohol are common too. But you have to be careful with that, otherwise, you'll be competing drunk.' He gave a chuckle, as though an old memory had flashed in his mind. His eyes then fixed back on Matthews, who was not laughing, so he continued. 'In truth, these are actually just used to treat aches and pains or fatigue. So you'd normally see these being taken after an event more than before. Some think taking it before the competition is a preventative, but I disagree.'

'What about after training? Would they be used then, or just race day?'

'Sure, if they're feeling the need to use them. With training usually increased in the lead up to an event, I can see many athletes being in pain and wanting to use them.'

'Do you think an overdose of these things could be a cause of death?'

'Well, yes, of course. You shouldn't need to be asking me that.' Basset raised his eyebrows. 'But any manager knows to only allow the team small amounts. You don't just let them take it when it's not needed.'

'Singleton says his team were not on that kind of thing as far as he knew. Do you think he would know if they were?'

'Bullshit he didn't.' Basset raised his voice. A passing woman looked at him, horrified, and he apologised to her. Lowering his voice again, he continued. 'As the manager, Singleton either gave it to them or told them what to get and where from. He's not stupid; he knows the game.'

'Thank you, Mr Basset. I believe you have been quite helpful in my investigation.' Matthews could see the train back to Whitby was preparing to leave, and with over an hour until the next one, he was determined to get aboard. 'If I have any further questions for you, I will speak to you on Friday when you're in Whitby.'

Mr Basset thanked the detective and made to leave the station. Matthews and Harvey raced aboard the train just in the nick of time as the train began to move a second after they had closed the door behind them.

'What now?' Harvey asked as he again watched the view from the window.

'We still desperately need to speak with Mr Ward, so we have to find out when he'll be available to talk to us at the hospital.'

'What about Singleton and Herdman?'

'They're too wrapped up in this week's boat race. Which is exactly what I want them to be focused on.'

CHAPTER 16

When Matthews returned to the police station that afternoon, he was surprised to see somebody sitting in his office waiting for him. From the outer office, Mrs Lloyd-Hughes beckoned him over.

'B-been w-waiting for you o-over an h-hour,' she wheezed, her cigarette balanced between her lips as she spoke.

'Who is she?'

'M-Mrs Fay Clark. S-says her s-son is…'

'Thank you, Mrs Lloyd-Hughes.' Matthews cut her off and walked into his office.

'Mrs Clark, I believe?' And she jumped with fright

166

at his sudden arrival.

'Yes, that's me.' Her voice was soft and timid. She wore rollers in her hair and had an apron on over her polka dot dress. 'I hope you don't mind my intrusion, Detective, it's just that I heard you were the one investigating our boy's death... and...' She quickly untucked a handkerchief from her sleeve and caught her tears before they could fall.

'I am, and may I say how sorry I am for your loss.' He retreated around his large wooden desk and took his seat. 'How can I help you today?'

'Well, I found some things in Robert's belongings. I didn't know if they'd be important to the investigation but thought you ought to see them in case they helped. Gossips are saying it's murder, but I don't know why anybody would do that to my boy.' She again dabbed her face as tears fell down her cheek.

'I'm currently looking into all possibilities, but I am grateful for your assistance. What items did you discover in your son's belongings?'

Mrs Clark began emptying items from her oversized handbag onto the detective's desk. The first item was a large brown paper bag. Inside, Matthews was shocked to see lewd photographs of women and a small book, which Matthews quickly realised consisted of rather raunchy reading. He wasn't sure why she was showing these to him; maybe she thought they were out of character for her son.

'I don't know where he got them from.' Mrs Clark looked absolutely horrified. 'Clearly, he's been hanging around with boys who are not in the least bit gentlemanly. I beg you not to tell anybody about that.'

'Mrs Clark, you may be surprised to know that most men your son's age have these kinds of items. I'm not shocked at all. Though I admit, I wasn't expecting to see this kind of thing in my office today.'

The next item handed to him from Mrs Clark was another smaller brown paper bag. This one contained coca leaves and syringes. 'Were there any other kinds of drugs in his belongings?'

Mrs Clark did not speak but placed an empty vial on the detective's desk. The bottle was unmarked. 'I don't know what was in it, but with those needles, I can only imagine.' She began to cry. 'I can't believe he would do that kind of thing.'

'Thank you, Mrs Clark, for bringing these to me. Were you aware of your son taking any drugs?'

'No. Does that make me a bad mother?' She howled.

'Of course not, Mrs Clark. Everybody has secrets, and children have always been most secretive with their parents.' As he said this, he thought about his own upcoming child. Would he know if his own son was taking drugs being his back? Would he know if his daughter was keeping some kind of secret from him? His becoming a father was slowly starting to daunt him.

'Then, there was this.' Mrs Clark slid a piece of paper across the desk to him. Matthews picked it up and read it to himself.

"Clark, if you or your team come near my team or me ever again, you will regret it."

'Do you know who it's from?' Matthews asked her. She shook her head. 'Do you have any idea what it might be referring to?' She again shook her head. 'Did Robert ever show you this? Were you aware of it before he died?'

'No.' She sniffed. 'But my Robert was a good boy. He wouldn't have done anything bad to somebody else.'

'Mrs Clark, did you know the other members of

the Friendship team, or the manager, Mr Singleton?'

'Not really. I met one or two of the rowers, but only briefly. I'd never met the manager.'

'Did your son ever talk about the manager?'

'Occasionally. I don't think he liked him very much.'

'Can you recall anything he might have said about him?'

'Nothing specific.' She stuffed the handkerchief back up her sleeve. 'I always used to think it was just general complaining. You know, if he'd pushed them hard one day. Sports managers are always pushing their team to work harder, ain't they?'

'I believe they do.' May I keep these items?'

'Of course.'

'Is there anything else you think I should know?'

'No.' She stood to leave. 'Thank you for your time, Detective. I will see myself out.'

Matthews stood, but she was already away out the door in a hurry. Mrs Clark had been on his list of people to see, so he'd been surprised to find her in his office this afternoon.

Matthews picked up the handwritten note again and read it over a couple of times. It was clear it had come from somebody from the other teams, but who? Was he going to have to interview all of the other team members too? He was starting to worry this investigation was going to be never-ending.

He left his office, carrying the note, and made his way out to the stables. He was hoping to find Harvey, but the stables were now empty of people. He returned inside and checked some of the ground floor office areas. None of the workers he spoke to knew where Harvey was. He hadn't given him an assignment, so where could he have gotten to?

Matthews headed back up onto the first floor, and this time headed for his father's office. He wanted to show him the note and get his advice. He knew that speaking with the final rower, Peter Ward, was the main objective, but what if Peter didn't survive? This note could be the best clue of a rift between rowing clubs, and if he was to interview all the other rowers, he would need assistance in locating them all. That was where his father came in.

Matthews walked into his father's outer office, where his personal assistant was typing away on her typewriter. In her mid-fifties, she wore a long black dress and had her dark greying hair tied up in a bun on the top of her head.

'Oh, Detective, he's with somebody right now.' She stood up quickly and raced around her small desk.

'It's okay, Mrs Singh. I just need to quickly give him something.' Matthews brushed past her before Mrs Singh could stop him. He opened the door to his father's office, and a shriek immediately came from within. Matthews stood there in shock, mouth open at the spectacle before him. A strange woman had been sitting on his father's lap, and upon Matthews entering so abruptly, she had shrieked and jumped off the chief as quickly as she could. Both the mystery woman and the chief looked flustered, and his father stood up abruptly.

'What on Earth is happening here?' Matthews demanded, louder than he had anticipated. He cringed as he realised how much like his father he sounded.

'Son,' His father walked around the desk, his tone more sombre than usual and his expression of humiliation. 'This is Miss Cooper.' The Chief tried to ask casually, yet his eyes avoided those of his son.

'How long has this been going on?'

'Oh, well...' He looked at Miss Cooper, who had gone bright red in embarrassment. She looked slightly younger than his father, with light brown hair tied up, and she wore a pale purple dress. 'We met about a month ago.'

'Unbelievable.' Matthews turned and left his father's office, slamming the door behind him as he went. Mrs Singh looked sheepish as he marched past her.

As Matthews walked out of the police station and made his way home, he came to the realisation that he wasn't angry with his father for moving on, simply surprised by the unexpected revelation. Matthews' mother had been dead now for over a year. Although he had never considered his father to be with another woman, he didn't oppose it. He was just in shock to discover his father canoodling with another woman in the office. He was saddened mainly by how he had found out. He wondered if Charlotte knew about Mrs Cooper yet.

When Matthews reached home, he realised the note he had intended showing his father was still in his hand. He folded it and placed it in his pocket. He had left work so abruptly that his satchel was still in his office. Despite not having the conversation with his father, he had decided he would sit on this evidence for a little while before reacting. His first port of call was, and always had been, speaking to Peter Ward, which was more important right now.

CHAPTER 17

TUESDAY 16TH AUGUST 1892

Grace was in the dress shops backroom, stitching together pieces of fabric that would become Beth's wedding dress. The back room was cramped, with a large solid wood table in the centre to work on and materials of all shades lined along two walls. A small window let in light from the courtyard behind. There was a tiny old fireplace in the corner of the room, which the owner never allowed to be ignited in fear of damaging the garments.

'It's looking beautiful already.' Beth squealed with excitement at the scarcely begun dress.

'This is just the underskirt.' Grace laughed at her

excitement.

'I know, but seeing the top fabric here makes me excited.'

'This fabric is gorgeous.' Grace replied as she ran her hand along the soft lace that would become the sleeves. She and Beth had been talking about the dress non-stop since they had had dinner together over a week ago. After lots of discussions about the design, Grace had finally finished the drawing this morning.

'Do you think it'll be ready for the wedding next month?' Beth asked, scanning the fabrics laid out on the desk. They had spent the last hour choosing which ones they wanted, and now laid out before them, Beth realised the amount of work ahead.

'I don't see it being a problem. You're going to be helping too, are you not?' Grace smiled.

'Of course.' Beth giggled. She had less experience in dress-making than Grace, but she had learnt a lot in the short time she had been working there. Grace was patient with her and made a good teacher. The shop owner, Joan, was also a fantastic mentor and was more than happy for the pair of them to work on the wedding dress between other customers.

'Oh, now, what do we have here?' Joan appeared from the shop floor into the back. 'Finally chosen your fabrics, have you?' She, too, began to handle the materials and feel their texture. 'Mind, it was a long time ago now that I got married. Never wore dresses like this to weddings back in those days. It was just whatever you had that looked nice. Not to say it wasn't special, and my mother spruced it up a little for the big day.'

'What year did you get married?' Beth asked her.

'Oh, it was the summer of 1842, and I still remember what was on the front page of the newspapers that day as well.'

'What?' Grace and Beth both asked in unison.

'Queen Victoria had ridden on the very first train just the day before my wedding. It was a big story, as you can imagine. Hard to believe life without trains anymore, isn't it?' Joan cackled to herself. 'What will they think of next?' She left Grace and Beth to their work and returned to the front of the shop.

Beth only worked in the morning on Tuesday, and so when lunchtime arrived, she was helping Grace pack away the fabrics.

'I can't wait for us to get to the fitting,' Beth

mentioned as she carefully rolled up the material. Grace stood and made to hand her another piece, but her grip failed her, and an unexpected dizzy spell caused her to drop the roll of fabric. The large roll crashed back onto the table, knocking to the floor scissors and pins. 'Are you okay?' Beth left the fallen items and leapt to Grace's side.

'Yes, yes…' Grace tried to push her away. 'I stood up too quickly is all. Nothing to worry about. Is the fabric okay?'

'It's fine, but are you sure you're okay? You've gone awfully pale.' Beth was seriously concerned about her friend. 'What is it?' She studied Grace, who looked sheepish.

'I hadn't told you, but I've been having terrible morning sickness throughout the nights. I'm feeling okay now, just tired.'

'Oh my goodness, why didn't you tell me?' Beth screeched. 'Sit down; I'll fetch you a drink.'

'Honestly, there's nothing to worry about. Let me help clean up this mess.'

'Sit down now.' Beth barked. She was determined not to let Grace brush this off. 'Now, leave that. I will put them away, but first a drink.' She disappeared into the next room where Grace could hear the clanging of glasses and cups. She returned moments later, empty-handed. 'Tea is on; I've made some for Joan too. Now you stay there while I put this away.' Beth was good to her word and tidied up the back room while Grace stayed seated. Once she had cleared everything away, she brought through a tray of cups and a large teapot. 'Joan, I've made some tea for us all,' Beth shouted through to the shop front.

'Please don't tell her,' Grace whispered to Beth before Joan walked in. Beth didn't have time to reply but gave her friend a subtle wink.

'How lovely. Thank you, Beth. Grace, your sister-in-law has an appointment soon. Would you like to take that?'

'Of course, Joan,' Grace replied, all the while seeing the concern on Beth's face.

As the three of them finished their cups of tea, the bell on the front door rang, indicating a customer had arrived. Joan instinctively stood and headed through to greet them. Grace made to clear away the tray, but Beth stopped her.

'I'll do this.' She quickly snatched the cup from Grace. 'You go through. It will most likely be

Charlotte.' Grace thanked her and headed on through to the shop.

'Grace!' Charlotte beamed with delight at the sight of her. Charlotte had arrived at the store with baby Hugo in a large stroller. Joan was already hanging over it, cooing at the tiny baby.

'Charlotte, how are you, and how is he doing?' She gave her sister-in-law a kiss on the cheek and then brushed up next to Joan to see the baby.

'Irksome and tiring, that's for sure.' Charlotte smirked. 'But I adore him.'

'I will let you ladies get on,' said Joan. 'Grace, I'm going into the back to work on Mrs Marsden's dress alterations.'

'So what brings you in today?' Grace asked.

'These.' Charlotte lifted a large bag of clothing she had placed on the floor beside the stroller and handed them to Grace. 'I could do with them altering.' Grace took the bag and was surprised just how heavy it was. Balancing it in both hands, she turned to place it on the counter, and in doing so, found herself engulfed in another dizzy spell. Grace missed the counter entirely and went crashing backwards onto the floor, the bag of clothing landing on top of her. Charlotte screamed, causing Hugo to awaken and cry, and Beth came rushing through from the back with Joan to see what the commotion was all about.

'Grace!' Beth cried out and leant next to her friend. 'Are you alright, Grace?' Grace opened her eyes and was dazed. 'Stay there. We'll call the doctor.'

'I don't need the doctor,' Grace managed to say, her words weak. 'I just need to sit down.' Joan began clearing away the dresses that now littered the floor, and Charlotte had a hold of Hugo, trying to settle him again.

'Are you hurt?' Beth refused to let her get up too quickly.

'I think just my arm on the floor.'

'What about your head? Did you hit that?' Beth panicked.

'I don't think so. May I please get up?'

'Absolutely not. You need to take a moment.' Beth hung over her.

'I'm so sorry, Grace.' Charlotte looked absolutely horrified by what had happened.

'Don't be.' Grace finally sat up, and Beth stayed close. 'I just lost my balance. I'll be all right in a minute.'

'Grace, you're pregnant, you're not all right,' Charlotte demanded. 'I think I should take you home.'

'No…' Grace started to protest.

'I agree,' Joan interjected. 'Charlotte, I'll go outside and see if I can get you a carriage. Beth, I want you to head over to Doctor Bennett and ask him to make a house call…'

'I don't need…' Grace tried to object.

'No arguments.' Joan spoke loudly to overpower Grace from stopping them. She then leant closer to Beth and whispered in her ear. 'And after you have spoken to Bennett, head on over to the station and let her husband know.'

'I heard that,' Grace said. 'You don't need to worry him, and I don't need a doctor.'

'Too late.' Joan headed out of the shop to call a carriage for her and Charlotte.

Two hours later, Charlotte and Hugo were still at the house with Grace. Charlotte had convinced Grace to get into bed and rest and had even agreed, against Grace's will, to stay with her until Matthews returned.

When Doctor Bennett arrived, he was followed

into the house by Beth, who was so distressed by it all that she refused to go home until she knew Grace was all right. The doctor talked to Grace privately. After discussing the morning sickness and the sleepless nights, he informed Grace that she was simply exhausted. He prescribed her some tonic to aid with the sickness and instructed her to rest for a couple of days.

'Did you manage to tell Benji?' Charlotte asked Beth.

'He wasn't at the station. They said he was out, so I left a message for when he got back.'

'It's fine. Honestly, you can both leave now,' Grace told them. Both Charlotte and Beth were perched on the edge of her bed.

'I'm not leaving you alone,' Charlotte told her.

'Shall I go downstairs and make us a drink, or would you like some food?' Beth asked.

Grace shook her head and smiled. 'Well, I'm pleased I have you two to look after me.' Grace squeezed Beth's hand. 'Even if it's not necessary.'

CHAPTER 18

TUESDAY 16TH AUGUST 1892

It was mid-morning when Matthews found himself pacing back and forth in his office. His waistcoat was unbuttoned and shirt sleeves rolled up for another sweltering day. The windows were wide open in an attempt to get some fresh air, but all they had so far achieved was to make the sound of seagull cries even louder. His conversation with Mr Basset yesterday was playing over and over in his mind. He mainly kept thinking back to when Basset had said. "As the manager, Singleton either gave it to them or told them what to get and where from."

Matthews was used to people lying to him in order

to cover up their crimes. He was also used to them trying to blame others. Yet this time seemed different.

He was again yet to see Harvey this morning and was beginning to grow concerned. His tardiness was becoming a problem. What could he possibly be up to that caused him to be so late?

Matthews was promptly drawn from his thoughts by a commotion coming from outside his office and down the corridor. He proceeded to the outer office and stuck his head into the hallway to see what all the uproar was about.

'Where the fuck is he!' Singleton was shouting at an officer who tried to stop him from going any further.

'Sir, I'm going to have to ask you to return to the main desk, and we can continue this conversation there,' the officer replied firmly.

'Matthews!' Singleton screamed and pushed against the officer in retaliation. Matthews emerged from the doorway into full view. His immediate surprise was to see that Singleton was covered in cuts and bruises, and his nose was bleeding badly.

'Thank you, Officer. I'll take it from here.'

Matthews approached them, nodding to the officer that all was okay. 'Follow me, please.' Matthews spoke to Singleton sharply and headed back to his office. Singleton followed swiftly.

'Oh, m-my.' Mrs Lloyd-Hughes gasped at the sight of Singleton and rummaged through her desk for tissues that she always had handy. She handed over a cluster of them to Singleton, who didn't thank her and continued into Matthews' office.

'Take a seat.' Matthews ordered him, and pointed at the wooden chair he was to take. Matthews returned to his own desk chair. 'Now, can you tell me what's going on here?' His exhaustion was coming out in his short temper.

'Fucking Herdman, that's what.' Singleton grimaced. 'Not settled with killing my team, now he's after me too.'

'You're sure it was Herdman?'

'I have fucking eyes, don't I?' Herdman fidgeted in his chair as though struggling to get comfortable. He balanced the tissues on his face under his nose and on the gash along his hairline. The day's heat was also causing him to perspire profusely, and his white shirt was dirty, blood-stained, and soaked in sweat.

Matthews noticed his terrible smell, both from sweat and alcohol. His eyes were bloodshot, and deep purple circles were beginning to appear around them from the fight. Matthews noticed that he also had cuts on his fists, a clear indication that the fight went both ways.

'Where and when did this happen?' Matthews opened his notepad.

'Just now. I was coming out of the clubhouse.'

'So, down the narrow lane?'

'Yes.'

'Did anybody else see this happen?'

'Probably not.' Singleton shrugged.

'And you came straight here?'

'Yes!' Singleton sighed. Matthews took out his pocket watch to check the time.

'Okay, Mr Singleton, I want you to go back to the front desk and get them to file a report. In the meantime, I'll speak with Herdman.'

'What? Is that it? I hope you'll be fucking arresting him. He'll deny it, you know. Fucking coward he is.'

'Possibly, but for now, I need you to file the report and...' Matthews looked at the state he was in, '...maybe see a doctor and get yourself cleaned up.'

Matthews stood and escorted Singleton out of his office.

'I want to see some action taken!' Singleton shouted. 'Arrest him, you incompetent swine.'

'Mr Singleton, enough!' Matthews raised his voice, though he immediately regretted it. 'Now...' He spoke calmly again, '...if you file a report, we can look into a charge for assault, but not until you do so. I, on the other hand, can look into how this ties into my own investigation.'

'Fine.' Singleton made it clear he was not impressed but refrained from saying anything more. The tissues pressed against his face were already making it difficult to talk.

'Mrs Lloyd-Hughes, if Harvey turns up, please inform him I'll be out of the office for the remainder of the day.' He spoke as he marched Singleton away by the arm. He took him back downstairs to the front desk, told the officer standing there to file an assault report, and left Singleton behind as he made his way outside. Matthews already knew where Herdman worked and decided to head straight there.

Whitby was busy as always, but today, as Matthews walked through the town, he was glad to see that coloured bunting and other outdoor decorations were being hung around the harbour, in preparation for the weekend Regatta. He had always attended the Regatta weekend since being a child. His family would always make sure to enjoy the whole weekend together. Each year they would hire a rowing boat, and his father would row while his mother sat at the back enjoying the ride under the shade of her parasol. As kids, he, and his brother and sister, would take it in turns trying to row, but the results would always see them going in circles, or with somebody getting wet. This year everything had changed; their mother was not here for the second year, his sister now had a baby of her own, and he had a wife and child on the way. It seemed to Matthews like an entirely different life. He couldn't help but reflect how life had changed so much in such a short space of time.

Wrapped in his thoughts, the walk to the end of Church Street didn't seem to take long at all. Matthews arrived at the W. Hamond Whitby Jet Shop, the largest shop on Church Street. With its sizable green shop signs with bright gold lettering and an impressive four window display showcasing various jewellery, it was undoubtedly one of the more popular and upmarket shops in town. Matthews had even bought Grace her engagement ring from this shop last year.

'Excuse me,' Matthews asked an elderly gentleman behind the counter. 'I'm looking for a Mr Herdman?'

The elderly man was smartly dressed, with his short white beard neatly kept and his white hair combed back smooth. Just like the interior of the shop, he was spotless and well presented.

'Oh, he's just popped into the back for a second; I'll get him for you.' He disappeared for only a second and returned with Herdman in tow.

'Detective.' Herdman walked around the counter to shake his hand. 'What a coincidence. I was planning on coming to see you this afternoon at the station.'

'Oh?' Matthews returned the handshake. 'Can I ask you why?'

'Somebody broke into the Jet Works Rowing Club last night.' He shook his head in annoyance as he spoke. 'I wanted to report it, and given your investigation, let you know.'

'I see. Was anything taken?'

'That's the unusual part. Nothing was taken,

nothing was broken… well, except the lock to get in. I don't understand why somebody would just break a lock and then leave.' Herdman looked genuinely stunned. 'I'm sorry, Detective. You came to see me about something?'

'Oh, yes.' Matthews cleared his throat. 'What time did you arrive at work this morning?'

'Around eight.'

'Have you left the premises at any time between then and now?'

'No. Charles can verify that.' He gestured back to the elderly man who was not concealing his obvious eavesdropping from the counter.

'Oh… oh, yes. He's been here on the counter all morning with me. Haven't even stopped for lunch yet, either of us.'

'Detective, may I ask what this is about?'

'Mr Singleton arrived at my office less than an hour ago; he'd been badly beaten. Said it happened outside the Friendship clubhouse and that he believed it to have been you.'

'Ah, I see.' Herdsman's face was filled with annoyance.

'Well, I can tell you it couldn't have been him,

Detective,' Charles interrupted again.

'Yes, thank you.' Matthews acknowledged him. Matthews had already come to this conclusion himself. Herdman showed no signs of injury himself, nor did his hands look like they'd been in a recent fight.

'Now, about your own clubhouse. Can I take another look at the place?'

'Of course, if Charles is okay with me leaving for a while.'

'Of course. Get going.' Charles beamed with excitement. This had clearly been the most exciting part of his day.

'I won't be long, then you can go for lunch,' Herdman told him and quickly grabbed his hat before following Matthews out of the store.

Matthews escorted Herdman to the Whitby Jet Rowers clubhouse. Once inside, the place was exactly as Matthews remembered it. The tidy interior looked almost museum-like, as nothing appeared to be out of place. After quickly looking around, Matthews was satisfied Herdman had told the truth and that nothing appeared to have been stolen.

'A new lock, I think,' Matthews commented as

they left the club. 'Thank yourself lucky this time. It's not common for intruders not to steal anything.'

'I'm convinced it was Singleton but couldn't prove it.' Herdman told him.

'Thank you for your time. Please do file a report about the break-in, and let's hope it doesn't happen again.' He left Herdman and headed on around to the Friendship Rowing clubhouse. He had no intention of seeing anybody but wished to simply perceive how private the narrow lane was. For Singleton to have been so severely beaten in the middle of town, without anybody noticing or hearing anything, seemed unrealistic to Matthews.

The lane led on down to the waterside, and the last set of doors was that of the club. Standing outside the Friendship doors, Matthews stopped and listened. The sound of the fishing boats and workers across the water could be heard. Back along the alley, the distant sound of people could be detected as a murmur. Surely somebody screaming would have been heard? As Matthews looked at the floor and walls around him, he noticed one key piece of evidence that contradicted Singleton's story. There was not a single speck of blood anywhere. For

Singleton to have been beaten so severely and turn up at his office covered in his own blood, there should have been specks of blood somewhere along the alley. So where then did Singleton actually get those injuries? And more importantly, why was he lying about it?

CHAPTER 19

Matthews had arrived at work late this morning, as he'd been reluctant to leave Grace's side. Having only found out about her collapse when he'd returned home, he was guilt-ridden not to have been there sooner for her. Charlotte and Beth had been a fantastic help. They even offered to stay later into the evening to help them both, but Matthews had politely refused and insisted they go home. He was grateful for everything they had done but could tell Grace was ready for them to leave.

This morning he'd been fussing over her for so long that he'd arrived at the office a whole hour later than usual. He was comforted that Grace was staying home to rest today. She had made him promise not to come home from work throughout the day to continuously check on her. So instead, he sent a message to Charlotte to check on her instead.

Conscious that he was unreachable yesterday, today, he found himself staying at his desk most of the day. It was early afternoon when he finally took note of the time. Typically, he would have been interrupted by Harvey long before now, but he had yet to show his face in the office.

'Mrs Lloyd-Hughes,' he shouted through the open door to the outer office. Within seconds, her tapping on the typewriter stopped, and she appeared in the doorway, cigarette still hanging off her lips.

'Yes, D-detective.' Her hoarse voice sounded worse than ever.

'Has Harvey been seen at all today?'

'I c-can't s-say I've seen him.' She began to cough, catching her cigarette before it fell to the ground. Her coughing had gotten worse too. Matthews wondered if her hoarse voice was sore or just a result of all the cigarettes she smoked.

'Odd.' Matthews turned to look out of his office

window. It overlooked the yard and stables. Though no longer a stable boy, Harvey was always down there whenever he got the opportunity. Whether it be lending a hand or generally visiting the horses. Matthews could see one of the regular stable boys, Anthony, grooming one of the horses and threw open his window to speak with him. 'I say, Anthony, have you seen Harvey at all today?'

'Not today, sir,' he called back. Matthews thanked the young man and closed the window. Mrs Lloyd-Hughes had already returned to her own desk and could be heard typing away again. Matthews had not given Harvey any errands to run today, nor had he asked him to follow up on any current leads, like he sometimes did. So where on Earth could he have gotten to now?

By six o'clock, Harvey had still not appeared, and Matthews was beginning to worry something had happened to him. He knew he wouldn't relax until he'd checked his young assistant was safe. As he left the station, instead of heading home, he headed towards the Church Street area in the hope of finding him.

The shops of Church Street were already

beginning to close for the day. As he passed Market Square, they too were mostly packed away and the stallholders heading home for the night. Matthews knew roughly where Harvey lived, though he had never been there before. He wondered if that was a bad thing; after all, Harvey had been to his house numerous times, whether invited or not.

As he proceeded farther along Church Street, he checked the names of all the little narrow passages between the buildings. Whitby was well known for having many narrow lanes that led to small yards, alleyways and ghauts, some of which were barely wide enough for a single person to fit through, and often a low entrance would cause even the average height person to duck. Matthews was aware these yards were dirty, dingy, and overcrowded, with multiple families often sharing small, cramped areas. Poverty was high in the town, and these small yards were usually the home to those worst affected.

As the detective approached the entrance to Argument Yard, of which he was almost certain was the one Harvey lived, he had a sudden dread in the pit of his stomach. He felt guilty, having never shown any interest in Harvey's living arrangements before.

True, Harvey was fundamentally a private person who preferred to talk about other things. Yet Matthews now wished he had taken more of an interest. He was also nervous, as police officers were usually not welcomed in these areas. He just hoped he wasn't walking straight into trouble.

As Matthews entered the yard, he was overcome with the smell. There was dirty washing piled up in the corner, the heap almost as tall as he was. Washing lines with pegged up clothes which were only slightly cleaner, swung above his head. A drain in the centre of the yard was blocked and overflowing with faeces. Despite this still being outside, the yard was so tightly packed and the buildings leaning inwards that barely any light made it down to the ground. Children of different ages, in various states of undress, sat around the numerous doorways. Some he knew would be orphans; others would have parents out begging or trying to get work. As he walked into the yard, his shoes made a clunking noise against the stone floor, and he could sense all eyes were watching him.

'Can anybody tell me where I might find Harvey?' Matthews asked, hoping that would be enough detail.

One of the older children, a young girl around ten

years old, pointed at a door tucked away in the corner of the yard. The door was hidden in the shadow of some stone stairs which led up to the second floor of accommodation. Matthews headed for the door and, upon reaching it, realised that the door was, in fact, ajar.

'Hello,' Matthews called out quietly, not wishing to make anybody jump. 'Is there anybody in here?' He carefully pushed the door wider, and it creaked loudly like a moaning phantom. Warm musky air from within hit Matthews in the face as he stepped over the threshold. 'Harvey?' he whispered.

'Detective?' came the timid voice of Harvey from within. A second later, Harvey appeared from around the corner. 'What ya doing 'ere?' He looked exhausted and had large circles around his eyes.

'You didn't show up to work today. I was concerned something had happened.' Harvey tried to reply to his boss but couldn't get the words out. Instead, he broke down in tears. 'Come now.' Matthews grabbed him by the shoulders, afraid he was going to fall. 'Whatever has happened, we can make it right again.' Harvey retreated back into the living quarter and beckoned the detective to follow him.

'It's my grandmother.' Harvey sobbed. 'She died this morning. I didn't want to leave her alone. I wanted to wait until the coroner had been, but he still hasn't shown.' Matthews entered the tiny room. A single bed rested next to a small fireplace, an elderly woman lying in it, motionless.

'I'm so sorry, Harvey.' Matthews had known Harvey to be an orphan and taken in by his grandmother. He had also learned that his grandmother had been mostly bedridden for the last couple of years. As Matthews scanned the room, he was heartbroken to see that besides the single bed laid out on the floor, there were more blankets made up as a bed. This was clearly where Harvey usually slept. 'If you like, I have a spare room you can take for tonight. I'm sure it would be better than being here alone,'

'Thank…' Harvey sobbed and could not finish his sentence. Matthews placed a hand on his shoulder.

'Has a doctor been?'

'I can't afford a doctor. I'd just been getting her something from the pharmacist to help with the pain.'

'Is it Mr Waters you're waiting for?'

'No, sir.' Harvey sniffled, 'I can't afford 'im either.'

'Well, I can, and I'm going to go and get him for you right now. Stay here; I'll be back soon.' Matthews left the lodging and marched back out onto Church Street as quickly as he could. Mr Waters, whose office was only a couple of minutes away, was more than happy to assist. He had a horse and cart outside Arguments Yard less than thirty minutes later. Matthews tried to talk Harvey into leaving, but the young lad refused to go until he knew his grandmother was safely in Mr Waters' hands.

'Pack anything you need for multiple nights,' Matthews told him once his grandmother had been taken away. 'You're welcome to stay with us as long as you need to.'

'But what about Mrs Matthews?' Harvey sniffed.

'Oh, I don't think she will mind. She likes you, and we can't see you staying here all by yourself tonight.' Matthews patted him on the back and offered to help clean up before they left. It became clear to Matthews that there was very little in the one-roomed accommodation, so there was nothing really to organise, and Harvey had hardly anything to pack.

It was after eight o'clock when Matthews and Harvey arrived at East Crescent, and as they drew near, he saw Grace was looking through the window, worried. Matthews had not wanted to be late home this evening, given Grace's recent incident. He certainly didn't want to spring this unexpected houseguest on her either, but he felt he had no choice.

'Where have you been all this time?' She kissed him the moment he walked through the door, her expression concerned at the sight of a downbeat Harvey.

'Nothing to worry about, but young Harvey here is going to be spending a few nights with us if you're okay with that?' Harvey stood next to the detective, looking at Grace for any flicker of annoyance, but to his relief, there was none.

'Of course. I'll just need to make up the spare bed. Come, Harvey. You can lend a hand.' Grace gave Harvey a warm smile and directed him towards the staircase. She quickly turned back to her husband. 'Is everything okay?' she mouthed.

'I'll explain later,' he whispered back.

'Come on then.' She followed Harvey up the

stairs. 'Let's show you to your room.'

Matthews was about to retire to the sitting room when a letter was posted through the letterbox. He recognised the untidy handwriting immediately and opened his front door to see a carriage pulling away. Opening the letter, he found it was from Doctor Bennett.

"I called in to see Mr Peter Ward at the hospital today. There is no change yet, though the doctor is more optimistic about his chances than when he was first admitted. With any luck, he should be available to talk with you within the next couple of days. Bennett."

CHAPTER 20

'How long do you think he'll be staying with us?' Grace whispered from the bed as she watched her husband dress. She didn't hide the fact she was admiring his bare torso from across the room.

'I'm not sure, but there's no rush, is there?'

'Oh, no. I didn't mean that.' Grace breathed, her expression turned to panic at the prospect of sounding uncaring. 'I just mean with the baby coming and everything, I'm sure he won't want to be up all night too.'

'Well, I promised him I'd help with the funeral arrangements, so once that's out of the way, we can look at helping him plan for the future.' Grace nodded. She was waiting for him to leave so she could dress and get herself ready for the day.

'You're going to take it easy again today?' Matthews buttoned up his shirt.

'Of course. Stop worrying and get out.' Grace laughed, and he strode over and kissed her. Her laughter made it difficult.

'I'll give Harvey's bedroom door a knock; I can't hear if he's awake yet.' Matthews gave Grace a final kiss on the lips before leaving the bedroom. Harvey had been put up in one of the smaller rooms at the end of the corridor, mainly because this was currently the only other bedroom that had a bed. Matthews gave a gentle knock, and upon hearing a faint 'come in', let himself in.

'G'morning, sir,' said Harvey. He was already up and dressed for the day in his officer's uniform. He had been unsure whether or not it was appropriate for him to leave the bedroom and head on downstairs, so he had decided to wait until he'd heard Matthews or Grace.

'Good morning. I hope you slept okay.' Matthews hovered in the doorway.

'I've never slept in a bed this big before.' Harvey smiled, though Matthews could tell this was not Harvey's usual cheeriness, but a muted version pinned with a tinge of sadness. Matthews nodded, though his mind returned to the image of the blankets on the floor, where Harvey used to sleep.

'I'm pleased you're comfortable,' Matthews awkwardly replied, never one for being good at small talk. Harvey, who had few possessions, had brought with him several ragged items of clothing piled on a chair in the corner, beneath which a pair of worn and shabby boots sat. On the bedside table, there was a brooch, which Matthews instantly recognised as belonging to Harvey's grandmother, now his only item left from her. 'I'll see the vicar later today to arrange a date for the...' He stopped himself, seeing Harvey's face fall. 'We should get going soon, I think.' Matthews quickly changed the subject. 'Looks like it's going to be another hot day.'

'Too hot for the horses.' Harvey tied his police boots' laces, which were in much better condition than his own old boots.

'Indeed.' Matthews was about the leave when he noticed something else in the room. 'I see you're reading The Police News Illustrated.' Matthews picked up the newspaper lying on the side. 'I haven't read one of these in a while; anything good being reported?' He scanned the front page, which was always covered in dramatic illustrations of crimes being reported from around the country.

'Just the usual,' Harvey replied. 'A wife's suspected of murdering her husband in Bristol. Body pulled from the River Thames, and a man who believes a ghost murdered his goat.' Harvey chuckled. 'The normal folly.'

'I remember, only four years ago, when this was filled with the latest gossip from the Jack the Ripper case.' Matthews threw the paper back onto the bed. 'Everyone around the country would be eager to read the latest copy and find out what had happened next. You would think they were waiting for the next instalment of a book series, but this, of course, was real.'

'Did they ever catch the killer?'

'No, but there are plenty of people who have their own theories.' Matthews smirked, recalling in his mind some of the more extreme ones he read. 'I, for one, think that after all this time, they might be too late. Anyway, we should get going.' He left the bedroom and headed downstairs. Harvey followed closely behind.

Upon arriving at his office, with Harvey in tow, Matthews compiled a list of jobs to keep Harvey occupied. The last thing he wanted was Harvey feeling upset all day and knew that keeping him busy was more than likely the best solution for the time being.

'Harvey, I want you to take the weekend off to enjoy the Regatta,' Matthews told him as he scribbled down random jobs.

'Ya sure?' Harvey sounded surprised. 'But there's still this case to finish.'

'I know.' Matthews sighed, frustrated that he had yet to close it. 'But I think it will be good for you to take some time off the case and work altogether. Mrs Matthews and I were planning to attend as many events over the weekend as possible. You're welcome to go with us. Unless you have some other friends, and you'd rather go with them?' Matthews stopped himself, realising he had no idea if Harvey had many friends, or indeed, any. How had he spent over a year with the young lad and managed to know so little about him? Matthews felt shame on his part.

'Goin' with you and the Mrs would be grand,' Harvey replied, though his expression was sad. 'As long as you're sure you don't need me.'

'Absolutely. You can keep Mrs Matthews company if I need to do any work.'

Matthews finished compiling the list, at the top of which was to visit the large pharmacy. After their conversation with Basset earlier in the week, Matthews now had a better idea of what kinds of stimulants athletes used. He wanted to get some more information on them and determine what the rowers and manager had been buying. Matthews also wrote Harvey a signed note, asking the pharmacist for details on various tonics and stimulant drugs they may sell over the counter. The pharmacist knew Matthews and Harvey well, so Matthews had no concerns about him handing over the information.

***

Scanning the list as he walked up the street, Harvey decided that seeing the pharmacist was the top priority. The pharmacist was located in Market Square. A large window overlooked the square, with a variety of coloured glass bottles and jars on display. This theme continued inside, with the entire wall behind the large wooden counter dedicated to bottles. Harvey enjoyed visiting the pharmacy, purely because the shop always smelt differently each time he visited. Today there was more of an earthy scent to the shop, as the pharmacist was sorting through an array of freshly picked plants, ready to turn into medicines and tonics. Fascinated by it all, Harvey could easily have spent hours asking questions. However, today, he knew there was no time and solely presented the note and got the required information.

After successfully managing to get all the information the detective required, Harvey decided to make a slight detour before continuing with the rest of the list. His old home in Arguments Yard was just around the corner, and Harvey wanted to get any last things before it was too late.

When he had packed in front of Detective Matthews, he had refrained from rummaging through his grandmother's personal belongings, and instead packed up mostly his own things. As he made his way into the dark and dirty yard, a young girl, no older than five, smiled at him. She was barely dressed and had bare feet, yet her smile was warm and genuine. He knew her since she'd been born.

Harvey entered the small, one-room lodging, and upon seeing the empty bed, broke down in tears. His grandmother had been laid there the last time he was there, and the thought of her no longer being with him had yet to fully sink in. Yet he knew he was now completely alone. His parents had both died when he was a baby, and his grandmother had been the only living relative he had left. His stomach churned as he wondered what would happen to him now. He knew Mr and Mrs Matthews couldn't look after him forever. The thought of being homeless was sickening to him. Many people were already homeless in the town, with little hope or help of getting out of their circumstance. He could just about pay for this one-roomed accommodation alone, but that would give him little left for food. Though a second job was not out of the question. Harvey's mind was going so fast that he began to get a headache. After composing himself, he began to search the room. Firstly, he stripped the bed and checked under the mattress. His grandmother was known for hiding things, so he wouldn't put it past her, leaving something under there. His instinct was correct, and a tiny amount of money was folded up in a dirty envelope. It wasn't much, but it was something.

Harvey pocketed the envelope of money and turned his attention to items under the bed. He found a box filled with paperwork. Most of it pre-dated his own birth, including a marriage licence for his grandmother, dated 1838.

Harvey knew his grandmother didn't have anything of real value but wanted to check through her belongings before disposing of anything. He didn't really want to come back and live here either, but knew it was a step up from homelessness.

At the bottom of the box of papers, Harvey found his own birth certificate. It displayed his full name, Harvey Paul Allen, and his date of birth, March 15, 1877. His parents' names, Colin and Eloise, were strangers to him, having been too young to remember them. He didn't even have a photograph or portrait of them, so he had no idea what they looked like. The final item in the box was a large envelope. Harvey opened into it and discovered two pieces of paper. The first was another birth certificate. Harvey read it twice, trying to understand what he was seeing. According to the paperwork, his parents had had another child, born six years before Harvey. His name, George Allen. Harvey came over cold. How had he never known he had an older brother?

The second piece of paper fell to the floor, and as Harvey picked it up, his stomach sank. It was a signed document stating that George had been handed over to the workhouse; the reason given, he was a child out of wedlock. Harvey fought back the tears as he reread the documents. It informed him that George had been born on February 7th, 1871. It also told Harvey that his parents had handed over custody of the baby on February 8th. George had only been a day old. Thus far, Harvey had narrowly avoided living in a workhouse, though many children who lost their parents usually did. He knew most towns and cities had their own workhouses, and Whitby was no exception. He had heard the rumours, as many of the poor community had. How could his parents have done this? Was his brother still at the workhouse, just minutes away from where he'd lived his entire life?

CHAPTER 21

THURSDAY 18TH AUGUST 1892

O nce Harvey had left his office, Matthews began working on his own list of jobs. The first was to visit the Church of Saint John the Evangelist, just a short walk around the corner. He knew the vicar only by name and hoped to arrange a small service for Harvey's grandmother. Matthews was aware that Harvey couldn't afford it, but thought it the least he could do for him. He also knew Harvey would need to find a more permanent home and that he would have to help with this at some point too. He contemplated asking Grace if Harvey could stay with them longer term but was unsure if that would be a good idea, especially with a baby on the way.

Leaving the station for the church at mid-morning, Matthews was engulfed in the heat of the sun. Even on the short walk, he could feel his face burning.

The church, which was positioned on the small junction of Brunswick Street and Baxtergate, was a large stone building with enormous stained glass windows. Despite it being a grand building in its own right, it was undoubtedly one of the more understated churches in town, with no great monumental spire or grounds.

After a lengthy conversation with the vicar, a small service had been booked for the following week.

'May I ask what you expect the congregation size to be?' the vicar asked as he walked Matthews to the door. He was a thin man, no older than fifty, with short mousy brown hair and large eyes with big, bushy eyebrows. He was wearing a smart shirt and trousers, a traditional clerical collar, and a silver chain with a crucifix.

'He doesn't have any family left,' Matthews told the vicar. 'It could be just my wife and I.'

'I see.' The vicar gave a smile, though it was evident in his eyes he was saddened to hear this.

'I will ask around at the station. I'm sure some of them will be more than happy to attend and support Harvey; he's well-liked. And I'm sure my father, erm... the chief will come.'

'Thank you, Detective.' The vicar shook his hand as they reached the doors. 'If there is anything else I can do before the service, please let me know.' Matthews thanked him and left the church. He couldn't help but think about how Harvey must be feeling. The last funeral Matthews had attended had been his own mother's. Yet, he was fortunate to still have his father and siblings for support. Harvey had nobody, and this in itself made Matthews more determined to look after him.

Before heading back to the station, Matthews decided to make a quick visit home. He had kept to his promise yesterday not to return and check on her, but today he couldn't resist. He had to admit that Grace already looked a lot better than when he had arrived home to find her tucked up in bed, though he refused to pretend he wasn't concerned about her.

'What are you doing here?' Grace poked her head from the kitchen upon hearing the front door. She beamed at the sight of him. Dusting off her flour-covered hands on her apron, she joined him in the hallway.

'Coming home to kiss you, of course.' He scooped her into a large embrace.

'Check on me, you mean.' She sniggered.

'Never.' Matthews pulled her in for another kiss. 'I can't stay long. Has Charlotte been today?'

'Not yet, but I wouldn't be surprised to see her. She's still shaken up about the other day. I've never seen her look so concerned.'

'Well, she cares about you, as do I.' He kissed her again. 'What are you making?'

'Just some bread. I was thinking of making a pie afterwards.'

'Yes, please.' Matthews pretended to lick his lips. 'Just don't go overdoing it.'

'I took a walk to the shop this morning. I saw Beth and Joan. I didn't stay long, as they had appointments.'

'They'll have been pleased to see you looking well.'

'Yes, though Joan has forced me to have the rest of the week, and Regatta weekend, so I will be plenty rested.'

'Good.' Matthews smiled. 'I always did like Joan.'

He beamed a comic style smile at her, and she playfully tapped him on the arm.

'You'd have me stay home every day, you would.'

'Not true.' He kissed her forehead and finally let her go. 'But I agree with Joan that you need to take it easy.'

'Well, I may have brought some of the fabrics for Beth's wedding dress home. I can stitch while seated here.' Matthews laughed. He knew she wouldn't be able to resist.

'I have to get back.' Grace walked him to the door and watched him until he was completely out of sight.

When Matthews returned to his office in mid-afternoon, he was surprised to see Harvey already there waiting for him.

'Is everything all right?' Matthews asked, walking into his office and sitting behind his desk.

'Yes,' Harvey replied, though his usually upbeat self had still not returned. 'I 'ave some information that I thought ya might wanna know.' He started to unfold pieces of paper from his pocket and placed them onto Matthews' desk. Matthews, who had noticed a small pile of letters, likely left for him by Mrs Lloyd-Hughes, quickly moved them out of the way to make room for Harvey's items.

'What's all this?'

'From the pharmacist.' Harvey was trying to lay them flat as they had been screwed up accidentally on his way back. 'It's the information ya wanted.'

Matthews began looking at some of the pieces, the handwriting on them difficult to read. 'So what did he tell you?'

'Well 'ere's the ingredients for all the tonics and whatnot ya asked for.' Harvey pointed at the majority of the notes. 'He says they're all regularly made up and dispensed, so nuffin unusual from his perspective.'

'What about the effects of use?'

'He said all tonics and remedies' 'ave the possibility of killing somebody if made up wrong, but said that, in his twenty years, he's never seen any of his customers die from his tonics.'

'What about over usage? That can be dangerous, surely?'

'Yes, but he says he never gives anybody more than a couple o'days' worth of anything, so they'd need to come back. 'e has it recorded who took what and when.' Harvey smirked, recalling something the pharmacist had said. 'He said, "ain't nobody going to outsmart me and my record keeping. I know everyone in this town, 'cos they all come to me for something." which is probably true since 'e's the only one.'

'Did he recognise the names I wrote down? Singleton, or the rowers?'

'He did, all of 'em, but said that doesn't prove anything as everyone in town goes to 'im, even you.' Harvey pointed at Matthews. It was true; Matthews had purchased from him many a time, more recently in the hope of helping his wife with her morning sickness.

'He was able to help, though,' Harvey continued. 'Said that Laudanum was always prescribed to Bert Ainley and Edward Walsh, as well as the majority of the workers at the dockyard they both worked at. He said they would use it to ease cramps and aches of the job.'

'Laudanum is here.' Matthews pointed to one of the scribblings on the desk. 'It's a tincture of opium. The list of ingredients is not surprising, but also concerning if taken in large doses.'

'But if the pharmacist kept track of people buying

it, surely an overdose isn't likely?'

'Perhaps, but that's if they were only taking laudanum, which I think we have established they weren't.' Matthews paused to think. 'We need to find out who they were getting other tonics and drugs from.'

'Do ya still think somebody tried to kill 'em?'

'There is unquestionably something untoward happening here.' Matthews replied.

'Are ya ready to leave soon?' Harvey asked, knowing home time was almost upon them. He had several other papers stuffed into his pockets and down his trousers from his grandmother's belongings. Harvey wanted to take them back to his new room to read them in better lighting. He had decided not to mention any of this to the detective just yet.

'I'll catch up,' Matthews told him, and Harvey left the office. Matthews folded away the notes from the pharmacist and placed them in one of his desk's drawers. He was still waiting to speak with Peter Ward, but he had yet to hear any updates on his well-being. He contemplated returning to the hospital to ask for an update in person.

Matthews glanced at the envelopes he had placed to one side and decided to put them in his bag to read later. One of the envelopes caught his attention as the wax seal on the back was stamped with a familiar-looking police crest. Intrigued, Matthews ripped open the letter and read it.

Detective Benjamin Matthews,

I have heard your time in Whitby has been going favourably for you professionally. I can barely believe that you left us over a year ago already.

I am, of course, aware that you were not altogether happy about leaving the city of York and your job here, and at the time, I told you there was little I could do. However, I am now in a position to be able to offer you a more senior role at the York Police department, should you wish to return to the city. I would be more than happy to discuss this further with you, face to face.

Yours respectfully,

John Howard Carlyle

York Chief of Police

'Ready?' Harvey popped his head back into the office, making Matthews jump.

'Oh, yes.' He forced a smile that even he could tell was fake and stuffed the letter into his bag for later. 'Let's go.'

CHAPTER 22

'Harvey, are you ready to leave?' Grace knocked on his bedroom door. It was the first day of the Whitby Regatta, and Grace and Harvey had planned on meeting Matthews in town at midday. Matthews, who had left for work as normal that morning, hoped to get some work done before spending the afternoon with them both.

'I'm here.' Harvey appeared in the doorway. He looked different out of his uniform. He was now wearing a pale blue shirt and pair of trousers, which Grace had made him last night. Grace had been surprised by just how little he owned, so she decided

225

to make him some new clothes, hoping it might cheer him up. He was clearly happy with them too, as his face beamed with delight upon showing them off to Grace, an expression that had not been seen in many days now. Grace was also dressed up for the Regatta, with a long summer dress she'd made for herself, a ruffled pattern which matched the colour of Harvey's shirt. She held a delicate fabric parasol in preparation for yet another scorching day ahead.

'Has Mr Matthews returned?' Harvey enquired.

'He's meeting us somewhere by the docks,' Grace replied. 'Shall we go?' She was concerned, as something about Harvey's expression seemed off. 'Is everything okay?'

'I need to show ya something.' Harvey beckoned her into his bedroom. Once inside, she was presented with an array of paperwork spread across the single bed.

'What's all this?' She leaned in closer to take a look.

'It was part of my grandmother's belongings.' Harvey sniffed but refrained from crying. 'I found my birth certificate as well as some other things.'

'That's nice, dear. You best keep them safe.'

Though supportive, Grace could tell he had more to say.

'I... erm... well, it turns out I...' Harvey was trying to find the words; he could feel his eyes filling with tears. '...I have a brother.'

'A brother? Grace was shocked. Harvey handed her the second birth certificate, followed by the workhouse document. 'Oh, Harvey.' She pulled him in for an embrace.

'Do ya think he'll still be there?'

'At the workhouse?' Grace looked back at the paperwork and realised his brother had been admitted over twenty years ago. 'I suppose it's possible. People rarely leave the workhouse. He'd be what, twenty, twenty-one by now?'

'Yeah, twenty-one.' Harvey interjected.

'I tell you what.' Grace placed a hand on his shoulder. 'Let's get to the Regatta, and we can talk to Mr Matthews about how we find out if...' She quickly glanced back at the paperwork, '...George is still there.'

'Okay.' Harvey's face lit up.

'Don't you worry, I'll help you find your brother.'

Harvey quickly grabbed Grace by the shoulders

and pulled her in for a hug. A range of emotions overcame them both, resulting in them now crying happier tears.

Ten minutes later, Grace and Harvey finally left the house. It was approaching midday, and they walked arm in arm down the gently declining Khyber Pass, a road cut into the cliffside, and made their way to the harbour. At the bottom of the Khyber Pass was an open area where a bandstand was positioned. This was a permanent structure and would often be the perfect spot to watch carollers in December or brass bands throughout the year. Today, however, it was where the town mayor was going to officially open the Regatta. The bandstand stood at the foot of the West Cliff pier, where deck chairs had been placed along the entire length for spectators to sit and enjoy the sunshine, as well as the passing boats.

Decorations in celebration of the weekend had been hung at the harbour, on the bandstand, and through many of the streets. There was bunting of varying colours, flags of various types, including the Union Jack and Yorkshire flag, and lanterns lining the harbourside and piers, ready to be lit upon nightfall. The majority of the boats had been decorated with ribbons and bunting too. It was undoubtedly a joyful sight to behold.

The harbour area was already crammed with an immense crowd, waiting for the official opening of the event. The crowds were tightly packed up to the waterside in order to see what was happening. An array of colours, as women were in bright summer dresses and hats. Gentlemen wore smart trousers and shirts, which were already starting to show sweat patches in the heat. All Whitby residents, no matter how rich or poor, would don their best attire for what was seen by many as the town's biggest event. Grace and Harvey edged their way through the crowd and found themselves a spot as close to the bandstand as possible. A small orchestra was already there, ready to begin. The atmosphere was of excitement, and Grace was thrilled to see Harvey looking so happy again.

'Good afternoon, everyone,' said a large gentleman with an enormous belly and a grey beard. He was well-spoken and dressed in a heavy smart suit, despite the heat of the day. His large gold chain of office hanging around his neck shone in the light. The enormous crowd that had gathered silenced for the mayor, Councillor Michael Wild. 'I would first like to thank those who have once again worked hard to arrange this weekend. It is a key event in our calendar, and year on year, we see a greater turnout.' The crowd applauded.

'Sorry I'm late,' Matthews whispered to Grace as he squeezed through the crowd and kissed her on the cheek. She gave him a smile and returned her gaze to the mayor.

'As always, we have a superb itinerary for you, including performances right here on the bandstand, plus there are stalls and street entertainers throughout the town.' He cleared his throat before he continued. 'There's a special demonstration by the lifeboat crew later today. The rower's race on Saturday, and not forgetting, the Whitby Challenge Cup yacht racing will conclude the weekend on Sunday, followed by music and fireworks.' Again, the crowd applauded. 'So without further ado, I officially open the 1892 Whitby Regatta.' A canon on the pier exploded, signalling the opening. The brass band began to play, causing the crowd to cheer the loudest yet.

With the mayor now gone, the crowd dispersed, and Matthews took his wife's arm as they made their way along the promenade and towards the centre of town.

'Charlotte and the baby should be coming down sometime this afternoon,' Matthews told Grace. 'We'll have to keep a lookout for her.'

'The baby has a name.' Grace laughed, poking her husband in the ribs. Matthews retaliated by merely pulling a silly face at her.

'So, what would you like to do first?' Matthews asked Harvey. Matthews and Grace knew this would be the first time he had actually attended the Regatta and wanted to ensure he had a magnificent time. Harvey would typically be working and so rarely saw much of the event.

'I'm not sure.' Harvey scanned the immense crowds.

'I don't think any of the boat races start for some time yet,' replied Matthews. 'So why don't we have a walk around and see what the stalls are doing.'

'Sure,' Harvey replied eagerly.

'I believe there's a Punch and Judy set up on Church Street too, so we could go check that out, and then maybe hire one of the rowing boats for a ride later?'

'Ooh, yes!' Harvey led the way, stopping at every stall along the route to admire the goods. Many of the stalls were similar to market stalls, with fresh produce, homemade jams and chutneys, and a whole variety of trinkets and homemade delights. Matthews and Grace realised it had been a while since they had enjoyed this kind of quality time together and were determined to enjoy their afternoon.

'Matthews!' a voice shouted from behind. He turned to study the masses and saw his friend Jack and his fiancée Beth hurrying to catch up.

'I wondered if we'd be seeing you two this weekend.' Matthews shook his friend's hand, and Grace gave Beth a peck on the cheek.

'You look beautiful, Grace.' Beth looked her up and down; her pale dress was undoubtedly stunning.

'Thank you, as do you.'

'I'm trying to stay hidden under the parasol.' She giggled. 'This heat burns me in seconds if I'm not careful.' Beth touched the side of her face, which already looked slightly pink.

'How are the wedding plans coming along?' asked Matthews, though, in truth, he knew most of them already from Grace.

'Extremely well.' Beth beamed. 'Your wife is doing such a splendid job with my dress. I may wear it every day of the week.' She giggled again, and Grace laughed at her comment.

'You must join us for drinks later today,' Jack suggested.

'Indeed,' Matthews promptly replied, glancing at Grace for approval.

'Of course.' She nodded. 'We're just headed over to see Punch and Judy with Harvey now, then maybe a rowing boat.'

'Oh, do tell us if he falls in.' Jack turned to Harvey, laughing but gesturing at Matthews.

'I will.' Harvey laughed.

'Charming.' Matthews smirked.

Jack and Beth wished them a pleasant day and continued on ahead of them towards the swing bridge and in the direction of Church Street. Grace had stopped at another stall before the bridge and was admiring some handmade pot-pourri. Harvey had joined her and was relishing smelling them.

'Have you smelt that one.' Matthews overheard them speaking as he took a few steps back to let others see the stall. As he waited for Grace, Matthews noticed his father walking up the street. Matthews hadn't spoken to him since he'd walked in on him and Mrs Cooper. He had been so busy with the case he had almost forgotten about that. Matthews raised a hand and gave it a wave in the hope of drawing his father's attention.

'Ah, I was hoping to see you down here.' His father's booming voice started before he was even by his son's side.

'Did you not come down with Charlotte?' asked Matthews.

'No. Told her I'd see her down here. Why, is she here?' He looked over Matthews' shoulder and scanned the crowd.

'I haven't seen her yet.' Matthews replied. 'Will you be meeting... Mrs Cooper, was it?'

'Oh, erm...' His father looked awkward. 'No, I don't think so. Promised to spend the weekend with Charlotte and the baby. I came straight from the station. Was hoping to get away for a couple of hours. I'll have to go back before the end of the day, though.' The chief pulled a handkerchief from his pocket and wiped his sweaty forehead. 'Anyway, I was hoping to see you because a message was delivered at the station soon after you left.'

'Oh, yes. From who?'

'One of the nurses from the hospital. She wanted you to know that a Mr Peter Ward has awoken and is responsive.'

'That's fantastic.' Matthews' eyes lit up, and he quickly took out his pocket watch to see the time, wondering if he'd be able to slip away for a little bit.

'Hold your horses,' the chief continued. 'She's asked if you can see him tomorrow. Says he needs his rest, but they're happy for you to go tomorrow, around midday.'

Matthews let out an audible sigh, disappointed not to be able to speak with him today. This was precisely what he'd been waiting for. Though another day surely wouldn't hurt?

CHAPTER 23

SATURDAY 20TH AUGUST 1892

Matthews had been tossing and turning most of the night. His thoughts continued to focus on the fourth rower, Peter Ward, and what information he could have to help the case. The rower's race was also taking place today, and Matthews knew it would be beneficial to see all the rowers and managers in one place. He was certainly expecting it to be a frosty interaction between them all, and as Matthews knew, this kind of hostility could often lead to more truths coming to light.

When Grace awoke, she discovered Matthews was no longer in bed beside her. The sun was only just peeking through the curtains, giving plenty of light to see that he had also left the bedroom. She rubbed her eyes, climbed out of bed, and tied her robe around her before making her way along the landing as quietly as possible in case Harvey was still asleep. She continued downstairs, where she found her husband in the living room, pacing back and forth.

'Is everything all right?' she asked, concerned by how exhausted he looked. The coffee table was littered with paperwork, and his notepad lay open.

'Couldn't sleep.' His reply was snappier than he had intended it. He paused, turned to his wife, and kissed her on the cheek. 'You should go back to bed; it's still early.'

'It's okay.' She yawned. 'Would you like a warm drink?' Matthews nodded, and Grace headed off to the kitchen. Shortly afterwards, Harvey appeared, startling Matthews, who had not heard him coming down the stairs.

'Mornin', sir.' He smiled, though he too looked concerned about the detective. He was already dressed, wearing his new shirt and trousers again, ready for another day at the Regatta.

'Good morning, Harvey. I trust you slept well

again?'

'Yes, thank you.' Harvey sat himself down in the living room window. 'Would ya like me to join ya at the hospital today?'

'Certainly not.' Matthews stopped his pacing and finally took a seat. 'You have the whole weekend off, so you keep to that.'

'If you're sure. I don't mind joinin' ya.'

'You enjoy your day with Mrs Matthews. I'll be along as soon as I can.'

Harvey nodded. 'Sir...' he cautiously began. 'I was hoping to talk to you about something.'

'Oh?' Matthews replied, though as he sat there rubbing his forehead, Harvey was unsure if he was really paying attention.

'It's about the workhouse.'

'Harvey, you don't need to worry. I won't let you end up in there. We'll sooner keep you living here than send you there.'

Grace returned with a tray, and Matthews quickly collected his paperwork away to give her space. Harvey decided now was not the best time to pursue his topic of conversation.

It was eleven o'clock when the three of them

finally left the house together.

'I'll try and catch up with you as soon as possible.' Matthews wished them an enjoyable day as they headed off in the direction of the harbour. At the same time, he made his way towards the hospital. The rowing race was due to begin at one o'clock, so he should have plenty of time speaking with Peter and still make it back in time.

Upon arriving at the hospital, Matthews was informed that Peter Ward was yet to see the doctor. Once this had happened, Matthews was then permitted to speak with him. Directed towards the waiting room, he found himself sitting in there alone. Matthews checked his pocket watch frequently, and each time it appeared little time had passed. There were newspapers in the waiting room, though these didn't interest him today. He sat there feeling more and more frustrated and apprehensive as the time went on. He needed to speak to Peter, but he really wanted to see the race, and more importantly, the managers. Every time a nurse walked past, he looked up, hoping he would be told he could go through. Yet each nurse just walked on by. Eventually, he picked up one of the newspapers in the hope it would distract him.

'Detective?' A young nurse finally walked into the quiet waiting room. 'I can take you to see Mr Ward now.' She smiled, and Matthews jumped to his feet and quickly followed her back out of the door.

'How is he doing?' asked Matthews as they marched up the corridor.

'He's doing much better,' the nurse replied in her high-pitched voice. 'The doctor thinks he could be ready to go home sometime this week. Here we are now.' She stopped outside a door with a small window that looked through into the private room. Matthews recognised this as the same room he visited only a matter of days ago.

'Thank you, Nurse.'

'He's going to be moved to the ward later today, but we decided to do it after you've spoken to him in case it's confidential… you know… given the case.' With that, she turned and headed back along the corridor. Her small, heeled shoes echoed all the way around the corner. Matthews knocked on the door and let himself in. As he entered the room, Peter's mother rose from her seat beside his bed. Without speaking to the detective, she squeezed past him and left; her pique expression towards him was less than impressed.

'Is everything okay?' Matthews asked Peter.

'I asked her to leave when you arrived so I could talk to you in private. She wasn't happy about that.' Peter had a much deeper voice than Matthews was expecting for someone with such a babyish face.

'I'm sorry. I didn't mean to cause any friction between you and your mother. I'm happy for her to come back if she'd prefer.'

'No, I think it's better we're alone. She'll only interfere.' Peter pulled himself up in the bed to sit upright. 'Please take a seat.' He pointed to the now vacant chair beside his bed.

'Mr Ward, can you tell me…' Matthews started as he sat down.

'Peter, please.'

'Peter,' Matthews began again. 'Can you tell me how long you've been on the rowing team?'

'I started two seasons ago. This would have been my third Whitby Regatta.'

'You are aware, I presume, of Mr Ainley, Mr Welsh, and Mr Clark no longer being with us?' Matthews spoke with caution. Breaking news like this could go either way, as he well knew.

'Yes.' Peter replied, quickly covering his eyes with his hands, he took a couple of deep breaths in order to compose himself. Even with his hand covering most of his face, Matthews could tell it was screwed up, and that he was desperately trying to suppress tears. Matthews gave the young man a moment to collect himself, and Peter eventually uncovered his face, and nodded to indicate he was okay to continue.

'I've been investigating the cause of these deaths, and over my investigation, I find myself talking to people who all blame somebody else. However, it's your statement that could really influence the final outcome of this case. Does that make sense?'

'Yes.'

'Can you tell me if you and the other members of the rowing team had been taking any performance-enhancing tonics or injectable drugs?'

'We were, yes.' Peter kept his gaze down on his hands, which were uncomfortably fidgeting.

'Peter, I want you to know that you're not in trouble, but I need to know where these came from and what you all took?'

'Okay.' Peter nodded but refrained from looking

at the detective.

'Can I start by asking how long you had all been taking these?'

'We started taking some of them last year. They helped with the aches and pains of training and race days.' Peter looked crestfallen as he spoke, shaking his head and fidgeting more as he continued to avoid the stare of the Detective. 'We quickly realised that taking them beforehand also helped. We'd only been taking them afterwards to begin with.'

'Can I ask what you were taking?'

'It started out as just coca leaves. You chew them and...'

'Yes, I know about them,' Matthews interrupted. 'They're cocaine leaves.'

'Yes, and then we moved onto some kind of tonic to drink. We would usually drink it after training or the race. This year we decided to try it before and after the race, just to see if it helped any.'

'Do you know what was in it?' Matthews quickly took out his pad and started jotting down notes.

'Bert said it had opioids in it, and cocaine, but I'm not really sure. It tasted terrible, but it really did help ease the pain. Though...' He hesitated.

'What?' Matthews encouraged him to continue.

'I found the tonic made me feel intoxicated. I didn't take too much before the races or training but would have more afterwards instead.'

'Did you take anything else?'

'About a month ago, we started on an injectable. I can't remember its name; it started with an L.'

'Laudanum?' asked Matthews.

'Oh, yes. That sounds right.'

'So you were chewing leaves, drinking the tonics, and injecting Laudanum. Is that everything?'

'Yes. Well, that's all I was taking, anyway. I had suspicions that Bert and Ed were taking more, but I couldn't be certain.'

'You say you only started injecting about a month ago. How often were you taking this? Daily? Weekly?'

'We started out taking it a couple of hours before the training or race. After about two weeks, we'd all started taking it daily, and that quickly escalated into multiple times a day, whether we were training or not.'

'You became addicted.' Matthews commented. 'What about the tonics and leaves? Were you taking more of these too?'

'Yes.' Peter sounded genuinely distraught. 'I was chewing them most of the day and taking the tonics every time I wanted a drink.'

'Peter, I believe your friends all died from an overdose, and I think you are fortunate to be alive.' Peter didn't look up. 'Can I ask you why you never stopped taking them after Bert and Edward died? Or why didn't you say anything after the poisoning allegation became public gossip?'

'I... well...' Peter was beginning to well up. 'I was scared. I knew I needed to stop taking them, but I couldn't. I didn't want to be blamed, so I kept quiet.' Tears began to run down his face, and Matthews handed him his fresh handkerchief.

'Okay, Peter.' Matthews could see he was distraught and knew it was best not to push him much further. 'Can I ask if your manager, Mr Singleton, was supplying you with these things?'

'No.' Peter was quick to answer. He wiped away the tears and finally looked Matthews in the face. 'He mentioned the coca leaves and said they might be worth trying, but he never gave them to us.'

'So these drugs, the four of you supplied them yourself?'

'It was Bert Ainley who came up with the plan. He had read somewhere that athletes were now taking things to help them better compete. He and Ed supplied the Laudanum; they'd been stocking it for a while before we actually started to use it. They thought it would be better to use it leading up to the Regatta rather than just training. So by the time we all started to use it, we had quite a lot of it.'

'So Bert and Edward were stockpiling ready for use in the lead-up to the Regatta?'

'Yes.'

'Where are all these drugs now?'

'Bert kept the majority of them at his house; he'd then give some to the rest of us at practice. I had a couple of weeks' supply but used the final amount the day I was admitted here.'

'When I searched Bert's house, there weren't any signs of Laudanum or anything else.'

Matthews suddenly remembered how suspicious Bert's mother had been and that something had clearly spilt on Bert's clothing after he had died. Clearly, she had disposed of the drugs to protect her son's reputation.

'Maybe he had gotten rid of it or something?' Peter

shrugged.

'Or somebody else did. So let me get this straight,' Matthews backtracked, 'all the things you were taking came from Bert and Edward?'

'Yes.'

'You're not trying to protect anybody?'

'Like who?'

'Singleton?'

'Nah. I wouldn't protect him.'

'Singleton believed that Mr Herdman had tried to poison his team. In the spirit of checking all avenues, can you think of anything over the past few weeks where you saw Mr Herdman, or if there were any opportunities he could have done something like this?'

'Herdman is not a very nice man, but I couldn't see him going to the lengths of trying to poison us to win. We don't see him, except at races, so I don't know how he could possibly do something like that.' Peter paused; his expression told Matthews he was thinking. 'If anything, I'd say Singleton was more likely to do that to Herdman's team.'

'Why?'

'Well, Singleton is crazy at times, and when he gets

something into his head, it usually drives him mad until he does something about it. Suppose he really is fixed that Herdman tried to cheat. In that case, Singleton will most certainly be up to something in retaliation. It's his nature.'

'Singleton came to my office a couple of days ago; he'd been badly beaten. Claims it was Herdman.'

'Has Herdman been beaten?'

'Why do you ask?'

'Singleton won't just sit back and let Herdman get away with it. If he thinks Herdman beat him and is adamant he poisoned his team, then I'd bet you anything he's not going to let it slide.'

Matthews swiftly pulled out his pocket watch. The rowing race was due to start in just over ten minutes. If what Peter was saying was true, he needed to get to the harbour as fast as possible. He might already be too late.

CHAPTER 24

SATURDAY 20TH AUGUST 1892

atthews thanked Peter for his time and quickly vacated the room. Before the door had even fully closed behind him, he took off along the corridor as fast as his legs would carry him.

'Sir, there's no running in the halls,' an angry nurse shouted after him, but Matthews had no time to waste and rushed past her at top speed. Peter's mother was outside the doorway of the hospital. Upon seeing the detective advancing her way, it was clear she wished to speak to him. Not wanting to stop, and before any words left her mouth, Matthews bolted through the doors and continued down the hospital driveway and out of sight.

The heat of the day was still suffocating, and running was making it much worse. Matthews was visibly sweating, yet he was determined not to stop. As he ran through town, cloud cover was starting to place the town into shadow. Along with a cooler breeze coming from the North Sea, it finally started to feel tolerable and fresh again, a feeling the townsfolk had not had in weeks now.

Approaching the harbour on the west side, he could see the crowds of people lining the edge of the water to watch the pending race. Thousands of people were all packed in as close to the edge as possible, stretching the harbour's full length and down to the pier. Matthews had never seen this many people in town before. Clearly, the gossip and newspaper reports of his investigation had drawn out more spectators this year.

Taller than most, Matthews joined the crowd and could see four rowing boats ready to begin in the middle of the harbour. Each boat had four rowers and one coxswain, Matthews instantly recognising Billy Forster as the Friendship team's cox. However, the rest of his team was new and unfamiliar to

Matthews. On the opposite side of the harbour, standing on Fish Pier, was the town mayor, who lifted a pistol ready to start the race. At the sound of the bang, the crowd cheered, and the four rowing boats began racing down the harbour, gaining speed as they made their way out towards the open sea.

As the four boats disappeared behind the enormous piers, Matthews' attention returned to the opposite side of the harbour. The mayor was now gone, and in his place stood three men he recognised; Thomas Singleton, Eric Herdman, and Jesse Basset. There was a fourth man on the pier with them; Matthews predicted him to be the manager of the fourth team.

From where he stood, Matthews could tell that Singleton and Herdman were having a quarrel and that Basset was trying to break them up. Matthews tried to break from the crowd and raced along the harbourside towards the swing bridge.

'Hey!' came a familiar voice as he raced across the bridge; it was Grace. She and Harvey had found themselves a spot on the bridge, a perfect position to see who would cross the winning line first. Jack and Beth were also there.

'Can't stop,' Matthews called and quickly kissed her on the cheek and handed her his satchel before continuing at speed.

'Is everything okay?' she called after him, concerned.

'Yes!' he shouted back. 'I'll see you back here.' He continued over the bridge and out of sight. The narrow streets on the east side of town were crammed full of people. With extra stalls along the road especially for the Regatta and visitors from neighbouring towns and villages, Whitby was the busiest it had ever been. Sandgate, already one of the narrowest shopping streets in town, was so crowded that Matthews could not get through in haste and frustratedly had to follow the crowd's flow.

Eventually, he made it to Market Square, where the crowd was less condensed, and headed for the narrow lane which led to Fish Pier.

'Detective,' came a voice from behind. He quickly turned to see Mr Welsh trying to catch up. 'Detective, can I have a word?' Matthews immediately recognised Edward Welsh's father.

'Can it wait? I'm in the middle of something,' Matthews continued to walk, but Welsh followed him to the alley entrance.

'I have to tell you something...' He was out of breath, '...something I did.'

'What?' Matthews asked impatiently.

'It was me,' he replied, still trying to catch his breath. 'I know Singleton blamed Herdman, but it was me. I beat the living crap out of that no good piece of shit... a couple of days ago, it was. I know he reported it to the station. But it wasn't Herdman; it was me. I was so angry that he had let our sons die. I wanted him to feel the pain we were going through.'

'Mr Welsh, you do realise I would have to arrest you for that kind of confession.'

'I... well... yes.' Welsh gave out a loud sigh, as though he was happy to finally get this off his chest.

'I need to get to the pier and see Singleton and Herdman now, but report to the station later today, otherwise, I'll have an officer come to your house.' Matthews knew this wasn't the ideal arrest, but he had more pressing matters to attend first.

'Understood.' Welsh nodded, and the detective turned to leave.

Matthews was able to slip down the narrow lane to Fish Pier. The four managers were all still here, though now none of them was talking. Singleton and Herdman stood apart, with Basset between them like a parent who had separated bickering siblings. Singleton was still heavily bruised all over his face, which made him look even more sinister.

'Is everything okay here?' Matthews spoke loudly over the increasing wind, and the four men all turned to look at him.

'Fine,' said Singleton quickly before returning his gaze to the water. Herdman didn't reply at all.

'Just your average rivalry, Detective. Nothing to concern yourself about,' Basset's deep voice responded before he too returned to keep an eye on the harbour entrance, eager to see which team would return first.

'How do you know they go all the way to the marker and back?' Matthews asked, trying to get the conversation flowing again.

'There's another rowing boat out to sea; that's the marker. Any boat who doesn't row around the marker is disqualified,' Basset replied without taking his eyes off the piers.

'How much longer do you think they will be?'

'Any second now.'

'Unless Herdman sabotaged my boat as well as my team,' Singleton spat.

'I never did anything to your fucking team; you probably killed them yourself, you attention seeking bastard. You'll blame anybody but yourself for your team being shit.'

Singleton charged at Herdman. The two men started throwing punches at one and another, resulting in a scuffle on the floor. Basset looked at the detective and shook his head; Matthews hastily jumped in to try and break them up.

'Are you not going to help me?' Matthews shouted at Basset.

'I've split them up once today already.' Basset grimaced. 'Got myself a fine bust lip in the process too. They're your issue now.'

Matthews forced the two men apart, both of whom were now winded and still laid out on the ground.

'Control yourselves, or I'll have you both arrested!' Matthews shouted, though instantly regretted his volume, which seemed to carry across to the spectators on the opposite side of the harbour.

'They're back,' Basset called. Singleton and

Herdman both jumped to their feet to see the rowers as they entered the harbour. The Scarborough Rowing Club led the way, causing Basset to cheer them on loudly. The newly recruited Friendship team was hot on their tail. Somewhat trailing behind was the fourth rowing team that Matthews didn't know about. Yet there was no sign of the Whitby Jet Works team. Herdman's expression was of quiet rage. The two leading teams swiftly made their way up towards the swing bridge, and once passed underneath it, the Scarborough team were declared the winners.

'Where the fuck is my team?' Herdman shouted, still looking towards the pier entrance, yet there was no sign of the Whitby Jet Work rowers. 'What did you do?' Herdman turned to Singleton, who began to back away.

'Nothing,' Singleton protested.

'You good for nothing bastard.' Herdman grabbed Singleton by the collar and dragged him to the pier's edge. 'What the fuck have you done?'

'Gentlemen, please...' Matthews tried to be calm but knew the tension had probably already gone too far. Herdman dangled Singleton over the edge of the pier whilst Singleton pleaded to be released. His wimpish cries were hard to watch.

'Herdman, enough!' Matthews called. He stayed back in the hope not to antagonise Herdman any further. It looked as though Herdman was about to throw Singleton off the edge when Matthews shouted, 'Look.' In the harbour entrance, between the two piers, came another rowing boat.

'They're back?' Herdman released Singleton, throwing him to the ground, and watched the boat come into the harbour. 'That's not my fucking team! That's the marker boat.' Herdman screamed.

The marker boat, which was smaller than the racing boats, only consisted of two rowers. Upon entering the harbour and guiding themselves out of the waves, they began to shout and gesture for help, not for themselves but for the final team. The cloud coverage had brought a coastal breeze that was causing the tide to become more turbulent. The marker boat was already struggling to control their small rowing vessel in the harbour entrance.

The Whitby lifeboat was moored next to Fish Pier. Matthews knew he needed to get their attention. Racing back along the pier and around to where it was docked, Matthews jumped aboard and pointed out the rowers calling for help. Within seconds, the crew was prepared and had cast away from the side of the boat. Not intending to have stayed on board, Matthews found himself joining them. The crew knew him well, as he had joined them numerous times when fishing boats and swimmers had been reported as missing. As they raced along the harbour, they stopped to speak to the marker boat, ensuring they were unharmed.

'What's happened?' Matthews shouted down to the tiny boat.

'There's something wrong! The other team, they can't continue. They all started vomiting,' shouted back one of the rowers.

Without another word, the lifeboat took off at full speed, through the harbour entrance, crashing through the rising tides between the two piers and out into the open sea.

CHAPTER 25

SATURDAY 20TH AUGUST 1892

The lifeboat turned out of the harbour and followed the coastline past the east coast's jagged cliffs, the ruined abbey and St Mary's Church and graveyard high above them.

'They shouldn't be far,' one of the crew members shouted to the team. 'Keep your eyes peeled, lads.' His name was Henry Freeman, the senior member of the group, and Matthews knew him well. An old friend of his father's and a local hero on the lifeboat. 'Put this on.' He handed Matthews a cork life jacket. The sea was becoming more and more choppy as they ventured out.

'Do you know how far they had to row?'

Matthews asked him, voice raised to be heard over the wind.

'To a point,' he shouted back. 'Let's put it this way, I'll know when we've gone too far.'

'I think I can see them!' shouted a younger member of the team, who was standing at the bow, balancing on the edge of the boat. Matthews was impressed that the young lad managed to keep himself steady and not fall overboard. He, on the other hand, was holding on for dear life as the lifeboat was tossed around relentlessly with every passing wave.

The small rowing boat was, in fact, in sight, and the lifeboat turned in its direction. From this angle, it was difficult to see if the rowers were all right, as the small rowing boat was caught in the growing tide. If they didn't hurry, the small boat could capsize in the waves, or worse, crash into the cliff with inescapable consequences.

'Eric, get the rope line onto the portside,' Henry ordered. 'Patrick, get spare life jackets.'

'Is there anything I can do?' Matthews shouted out to him, the wind carrying his voice.

'You can help me pull them aboard,' Henry

shouted back. 'Colin, you'll be dropping down onto the rower.'

'Yes, sir,' Colin replied and assisted Eric with the ropes.

The lifeboat was getting closer and closer to the precipice, and this in itself was a concern. Jagged rocks everywhere could cause insurmountable damage to the lifeboat, or worse, run them aground.

'Get ready, men. This is going to be close to the rocks. We will only have one chance before we need to pull back.'

Colin tied a second rope around his waist, and with Eric's help, he dangled over the edge of the vessel as they approached the small rower. All four rowers appeared to be unconscious by now, yet the cox was shouting and waving in distress. Eric threw a rope to the cox, who successfully caught it the first time, and together they were able to pull the rowers closer to the lifeboat.

'Pull us away!' Henry shouted, realising the rocks were a matter of metres away. The engine roared, and the propellers threw water in the direction of the rowing boat, unsteadying it further.

'Hold on!' Eric shouted down to the cox. As the

rowing boat got within feet of the lifeboat, Colin jumped overboard and climbed into the rower's boat. The lightest of the lifeboat team, Matthews could instantly see why Colin had been given this particular task. The rowing boat was finally secured to the side of the lifeboat, and Colin, with the help of the cox, began passing up the lifeless bodies of the four rowers. Matthews and Henry were there to pull them aboard, which was not an easy task in the wave-rocking vessel.

One by one, the rowers were heaved onboard, ending with Matthews grabbing the arm of the cox and hoisting him onto the lifeboat. Using the rope tied to his waist, Henry pulled Colin back aboard just in time as the lifeboat jolted, causing the rowing boat to detach, and there was an enormous bang.

'Get us the fuck outta here!' Henry shouted. The lifeboat had entered shallow waters beside the cliffs, and rocks beneath the surface now became a real threat. The rowers' boat took the worst of the beating, and between the waves and rocks began to break. The lifeboat roared into life. It managed to be navigated back away from the shallows and into the stormy open water once more.

Matthews instinctively assisted one of the unconscious men, as did Henry and two other team members. The lifeboat crew had been trained in first aid techniques, and Matthews had asked them to teach him some just a matter of months ago, should an incident like this occur.

The young man Matthews attended was breathing, yet he had vomited down himself and was ghostly pale.

'We need to get these men to a hospital as quickly as we can,' Matthews said, looking up to see what was happening with the other men. Henry wasn't listening but giving mouth to mouth to one of the young men.

'This one's breathing,' Eric shouted to Matthews as he hovered over another one of the rowers. Patrick appeared again with blankets and more life jackets for the unconscious men. Matthews quickly wrapped one around the young man he knelt beside, content the other three motionless men were okay until they reached the shore. The crew watched Henry as he repeatedly tried to help the rower, who still wasn't breathing. The waves threw them around, but Matthews could see the piers coming back into view.

'Do you know what happened to them?' The cox

asked Matthews, a distressed tone to his voice.

'I think this has to do with Singleton,' Matthews replied.

'But Herdman didn't kill the Friendship team, did he?' Matthews found the young lad's hesitation alarming.

'No, he didn't. But Singleton still believes he did.' An enormous tide hit the side of the boat, causing everyone to fall or stumble to the side. Matthews quickly grabbed the young man laid out in front of him in the hope of not causing him any more injury.

'He's breathing.' Henry eventually spoke. The young man he had been reviving spat up a mass of seawater, closely followed by vomit. Shaken by this sudden awakening, he began to shiver and was confused by what was going on. 'It's okay, you're safe,' Henry soothed the lad and began to wrap him in the blanket.

The tide was again rough in the harbour entrance, and all passengers had to hold on tight as they passed through the two piers. As they made their way up the harbour, the crowds of people were still intense and cheered the lifeboat and their crew upon seeing them return successfully.

Once docked, Matthews assisted in carrying one of the young men off the lifeboat with Patrick's help. They were pleased to see medical assistance already there to help.

'What the fuck happened?' Herdman rushed over and grabbed the cox by the shoulders. The cox began explaining everything to the club manager. While he was retelling the tale, Matthews' attention was momentarily drawn back to Fish Pier, just a short distance away. He could see the other teams and their managers still standing there, watching the lifeboat just like the rest of the crowd. Matthews' eyes caught those of Mr Singleton. He was pleased he was still around, as it was time to make an arrest. Singleton spotted Matthews looking over in his direction, and his relaxed expression turned to wide-eyed panic at the realisation Matthews was looking directly at him. Singleton backed away from the others on the pier, his gaze flitting around as he looked for an escape route; then with little in the way of hiding his intentions, he bolted from the pier as quickly as he could.

Chapter 26

Matthews charged off the landing dock, pushed his way passed the medical assistance, and raced on towards Fish Pier. Singleton had already disappeared into the narrow passage, which led back onto the streets of Whitby. Matthews dashed through one of the other alleys in the hope of catching up with him.

Reaching Market Square, Matthews scanned the hundreds of people still jam-packed into the streets. Singleton was nowhere to be seen, yet the detective knew he had to have come through this way. Trying to push his way into the crowd, Matthews intended to get farther into the square, constantly looking over everybody's head in the hope of spotting Singleton.

'Singleton!' Matthews shouted above the crowd, immediately recognising the back of the head of a man pushing through the masses of people. Singleton turned, his face filled with fear and adrenaline. Seeing the detective gaining on him and the crowd in front at a standstill, Singleton launched himself into the nearest market stall, causing the products and the stallholder to go flying. He began shouting for people to move out of his way, triggering the crowd to gasp, and a frenzy of fear broke out, causing those closest to Singleton to panic and try to flee.

Now trying to fight his way through a hysterical crowd, Matthews pushed through more forcefully and made it to the stall. The owner was now back on her feet, but Singleton had already made it through the square's remaining stalls, knocking over the owners and their produce in the process. He had now reached Church Street and could be seen fighting his way through the throng of people.

Matthews bolted through the constricted space between the stalls in pursuit, approaching Church Street and the mass of people Singleton had pushed to the ground in order to escape.

Aware of the detective's chase, the trampled crowd allowed Matthews that extra space to cut through them a lot quicker than Singleton, and Singleton knew this. Constantly looking back on his pursuer, his panic-struck face became more and more desperate. Singleton knew he just needed to hold the detective off a little longer with a break in the crowd coming. It looked as though luck was on his side as the detective tripped over one of the fallen crowd members, crashing onto the cobbled road himself with an almighty smack. The onlookers gasped and went to the detective's aid, with an elderly gentleman offering his hand to Matthews to help him back to his feet.

Slightly winded, and with a pain running across his shoulders, the detective sprang back to his feet, blood now running down his face from a gash on his forehead. Singleton had gained a further advantage and was now reaching the end of the street. Matthews ran as quickly as he could through the remaining crowd. By now, Singleton had already reached the end, and as he turned right onto Bridge Street, he disappeared from view.

When Matthews finally made it to the end of

Church Street, he turned onto Bridge Street, but there was no sign of Singleton. Where could he have gone?

'Detective!' shouted an elderly woman. 'He went down there.' She pointed to the narrow Grape Lane, a small street off to the left-hand side before reaching the Swing Bridge.

'Thank you.' Matthews breathlessly replied as he continued running towards Grape Lane. This street was still busy but nowhere near as bad as Church Street had been. The detective instantly spotted Singleton in the distance, fumbling with a set of keys, trying to open a door. Beyond Singleton was a uniformed officer.

'Officer!' Matthews shouted down the street. His voice echoed off the closely-packed buildings. The officer immediately recognised Matthews and started to jog towards him, both he and Matthews now closing in on Singleton.

Singleton unlocked the door in a fluster and pushed his way inside quickly, turning to slam the door behind him as briskly as he could.

'Not so fast.' Matthews' heavy boot blocked the door from shutting, and Singleton tried again to slam the door against it. With the help of the uniformed officer, Matthews barged the door open. Singleton took a swing for the detective, though Matthews was ready and avoided the attack, returning his own fist into Singleton's stomach, winding him, and knocking him to the ground.

'Thomas Singleton.' Matthews stood over him as the uniformed officer restrained Singleton in handcuffs. 'I am arresting you on suspicion of poisoning the Whitby Jet Works rowing team, with intent to murder, resisting arrest, and attacking an officer.'

'Fuck you!' Singleton spat at the detective. 'Why are you not arresting Herdman? He poisoned my team. He attacked me in the street! Why is that bastard still walking free?'

'I'm afraid, Mr Singleton, your accusations are false.' Matthews searched his pockets for a handkerchief to place on his still bleeding forehead. 'Mr Herdman was not responsible for the death of your team. Bert Ainley and Edward Welsh were responsible for that. Regarding your recent attack, I have also had a full confession from another gentleman, so Herdman is clear.'

'What?' Singleton sounded surprised. He was still

out of breath from running and looked to be in pain from Matthews' punch.

'I also believe that you weren't attacked outside the rowing club, as you reported, and that you were trying to frame Herdman for that in the hope it would make him look guiltier for the death of your team.' Matthews' voice oozed authority as he spoke.

'I…' Singleton lowered his head and decided against what he was about to say.

'I was able to speak with your fourth rower earlier today, Mr Peter Ward, who was able to confirm they had all been taking quite a lot of things to help them win the race for you. They were fed up with the way you treated them, and they thought if they won, they wouldn't have to be at the end of your anger. Sadly for them, they got addicted and went too far. Overdose is a common killer, I'm afraid, though I've never seen it in an entire sports team before.'

'What are we doing with him?' the uniformed officer enquired.

'Keep him here, make sure he can't escape, and I'll return with a carriage for him to be taken away in. We hardly want to be walking him through the crowds in handcuffs during the Regatta.'

Once he knew Singleton had been thoroughly restrained, Matthews left the doorway and returned to the main street, where he came across another officer patrolling. He told the officer about the arrest and requested he returned to the station with orders to send a carriage. Matthews then returned to the doorway and waited for the carriage to arrive. The uniformed officer guarded the door, and Matthews remained inside with Singleton sitting at the bottom of a stairwell, his hands behind his back in cuffs.

'Where are you taking me?' Singleton's voice echoed up the stairs. His breathing was starting to return to normal.

'To the police station. You will be held overnight and be taken in for questioning.'

'By you?'

'No.'

'How's Peter?'

'Lucky to be alive, unlike his teammates.'

'I knew about the coca leaves...' Singleton began.

'Save it for the interview.' Matthews told him.

'I knew about the tonics too. I told Bert which ones were better.'

'Singleton, stop. Save it for the station.'

'I told Ed about the Laudanum too... but I didn't expect them to take them all in one go. The fools,' Singleton mumbled to himself, his face grimaced in fury, and veins began to bulge in his forehead as he got angrier and angrier. Matthews stayed silent. Out of the blue Singleton's expression changed, and the anger eased into panic. He looked up at Matthews wide eyed and fearful. 'Do you...' Singleton sniffed, '...think they will hang me?'

'I don't know.' Matthews replied. Though in truth, he had seen men hang for less.

'The carriage is here.' The uniformed officer peered back into the doorway. Singleton was then escorted down Grape Lane by Matthews and the officer. He was placed into the back of the carriage, where the uniformed officers took him away.

Returning to the dockside, Matthews searched the crowds for Grace and Harvey, though they weren't where he'd left them. He recognised he'd been longer than expected. There was still plenty of the day left, and although he would need to return home first to change out of his blood-stained shirt, he was hopeful he could still relish in some Regatta fun with Grace and Harvey.

'Matthews,' came a familiar voice. It was Jack. 'What the hell happened? You're covered in blood.' His eyed darted from Matthews' blood covered forehead to his blood covered shirt; Matthews didn't realise he looked that bad.

'Just a graze. I'll be fine.' Matthews dabbed his forehead again, which was now mostly just covered in dried up blood. 'Where have Grace and Beth gone?'

'Grace was feeling unwell; she nearly fainted, so Beth helped her home.' Matthews' face fell, and he swiftly took off in the direction of home.

'Thank you!' Matthews called back to his friend.

A couple of minutes later, exhausted and out of breath, Matthews charged through his front door, where he immediately heard screams of distress coming from upstairs.

'Grace!' he shouted and raced up the stairs, two at a time. As he entered the bedroom, he found Grace hunched over on the floor, Beth beside her, trying to calm her. Grace's face was wet with tears and sweat, and her sobbing and cries of pain chilled Matthews to the bone.

'Benji…' she called out to him, 'I'm sorry.' She

held out a hand for him, and he took it gently, scared of hurting her. It was then he saw that the front of her dress which was drenched in blood.

'What's happened? Have you called for the doctor?' His voice trembled; his eyes filled with tears. Grace screamed again and recoiled in pain.

'Harvey has gone for Doctor Bennett,' Beth replied, still holding Grace close. 'Though it's probably not going to be good news about the baby.'

EPILOGUE

THURSDAY 25TH AUGUST 1892

Quiet filled the house this morning. It had seemed as though it had been like this for days now. No visitors had called today, unlike previous days and Matthews, Grace and Harvey had barely left the solitude of the house since the weekend.

Matthews could be heard pacing in the sitting room. His shoes against the wooden floor echoed through the house. Grace was in her bedroom, getting into the black dress she had spent the morning repairing a small hole in the seam. Harvey, who was already dressed and ready for the day laid on his bed. He was surrounded by the documents in which he endlessly poured over each day. His emotions zipping constantly between sadness and anger. The letter in his hand, a new addition to his pile.

Dear Detective,

Upon receiving your letter, I was familiar with the name George Allen, and after looking into this, I can now say I remember him well.

George was eight years old when my husband and I arrived to take over the workhouse and was one of the more hard-working and upbeat characters. I can tell you that George is no longer with us here at Whitby, and was moved to the workhouse in Thirsk, in 1884, when he was around thirteen years old. This was due to overpopulation at our own workhouse, and orphaned children were sent to those with spaces.

I'm unaware if George is still at Thirsk, but you should speak with the matron there, Mary Jane Dawson.

Sincerely yours,

Isabella Watson (Matron)

Harvey had read and re-read the letter so many times since Matthews had given it to him yesterday that he almost knew it by heart. Though the detective and Grace had promised to help him continue to search for his brother, Harvey couldn't help but feel sad that he hadn't been found in time for his grandmother's funeral today.

'Hervey?' Grace's voice came from outside the bedroom door, followed by a gentle knock. 'Are you ready to leave soon?'

'Come in!' Harvey shouted, and Grace let herself in. She was wearing a long elegant black dress, with a small hat. Her face lit up at the sight of Harvey. He was sitting on the edge of his bed wearing his smart police uniform, a decision he knew his grandmother would have approved of.

'It's time to leave.' Grace held out a hand for him, which Harvey took it without hesitation, and followed her back out onto the landing.

'What 'bout you?' Harvey asked as they descended the stairs. 'You okay?'

'I'm here for you today. Don't you worry about me.' She gave his hand a squeeze.

The ceremony this morning, at the Church of Saint John the Evangelist, was short. Harvey decided he didn't want to make any kind of speech and that the vicar could choose the hymns. Upon seeing the coffin, Harvey felt his mouth go dry and his palms sweaty. Grace, who sat next to him during the service, kept looking at him and giving him a reassuring smile, which instantly comforted him.

When the service was over and guests began to head for the exit, Harvey instead walked up to the altar. His first stop was to take a closer look at the closed coffin. He had not shed a tear at all today, and he wondered why. Had he used up all of his tears after his grandmother's death? Or was he still in a state of denial about it all?

Before leaving the church, Harvey made to speak with the vicar. He didn't have much to say but simply wished to thank him for the service.

'She would'a never 'ave expected a send-off like that,' he told the vicar, who was happy that Harvey was so grateful. As he spoke to the vicar, he saw Matthews and Grace waiting for him at the doors. A handful of guests talking to them.

'Thank you so much for coming. I know Harvey was pleased to see you.' Matthews shook Jack's hand and gave Beth a kiss on the cheek. Matthews had asked them if they would attend Harvey's grandmother's funeral, concerned that the church would be empty. Yet to Matthews' surprise, a handful of residents from Arguments Yard had attended the service, sitting at the back of the church. Some of the younger police force who knew Harvey had also come out to show their support too. Even Matthews' father, the police chief, had made a special trip to the church for the service.

'Not at all,' Jack replied. 'He's a great kid, and it's always good to be surrounded by people for support during these things.'

Jack and Beth turned to walk out of the large gothic doors of the church. Beth turned back to speak again before they left.

'By the way, Grace, you're looking well today. I hope we can catch up soon.'

'Certainly. We'll need a dress fitting for you. The wedding must be only two weeks away now.'

'Indeed.' Beth gave an excitable smile, though quickly stopped herself at the sight of Harvey, who was approaching. She and Jack wished Harvey well and made to leave.

'Thank you for everything you've done today.' Harvey held out his hand to shake Matthews'. 'I wish I could repay ya somehow.'

'Don't think about it.' Matthews returned the handshake.

'And Mrs Matthews, thank you for coming. I know it's been a tough week for ya.' He gave Grace a big hug. Matthews and Grace couldn't believe how tall he was now getting, equalling Grace in height, if not taller.

'I couldn't let you down today.' Grace ruffled his hair and smiled warmly at him.

She had admittedly been nervous about today for her own personal reasons. For today had been the first time she had left the house since her miscarriage. The physical pain had gone, but the emotional anguish still remained. Having been at home since the incident, she had been worrying about leaving the house for days, dreading the sympathy and sad faces she knew she would have to deal with. Just a further reminder of her loss. Despite these worries, most people had been kind to her and allowed the day to be rightfully about Harvey and his grandmother.

'Good show, Harvey.' Matthews' father's voice boomed as he made his way out of the church. 'Superb send-off. You have done her proud.'

'Thank you,' Harvey replied, and the chief patted

him on the back before heading off back to the police station.

'Shall we head home then?' Matthews asked Harvey and Grace. Matthews had made the decision to take the entire day off. His latest case had been closed, and today was all about Harvey.

'Oh, by the way…' the chief re-appeared. 'I completely forgot.' He huffed and puffed as he walked back to their side. 'Harvey, I hear you're temporarily living with my son, is that correct?'

'Just until he can get back on his feet,' Matthews interjected.

'Yes, yes,' the chief scoffed. 'Well, there is a small living compartment over the stables at the police station. Used to be occupied by Cecil Owen, the old stable hand, before he died. Hasn't been lived in for quite some time mind you, so will no doubt need cleaning up a lot, but you're welcome to take that if you'd like?'

'Oh, sir.' Harvey was speechless.

'How about we take a look at it over the weekend,' said Matthews. 'If it's that bad, you can stay with us while we get it cleaned up for you.'

'That sounds perfect. Thank you, Detective, and

thank you, Chief.' Harvey was starting to tear up. In fact, Matthews and Grace had not seen a smile on his face so wide for some time.

'Time for home, I think.' Grace grabbed Harvey by the hand. 'A nice dinner is what we all need after today.'

Matthews, Grace, and Harvey all made it back to the house twenty minutes later. Harvey followed Grace straight into the kitchen to help prepare dinner. Matthews, who wasn't technically working today, took his work bag off the dining room table and took it to hang on the hat stand by the front door. He tossed it over one of the hangers but missed, and the satchel fell to the ground. As he picked it up, a piece of paper fell out. He unfolded it and instantly recognised what it was. He'd completely forgotten about the letter from the York police chief. He had yet to respond to it, and with everything that had been going on, hadn't even spoken to Grace about it yet. Re-reading the letter, Matthews knew that he would have jumped at the offer to return to York a year ago, but now things had changed. He was married and was enjoying being closer to his sister and Jack. Then, of course, there was Harvey. Matthews was surprised by how protective of him he had become. Yet after the distressing couple of weeks he, Grace, and Harvey had had, maybe a new start in the city was exactly what they needed.

'What's this?' Grace had returned from the kitchen without Matthews realising. He handed her the letter, which she quickly read. 'Oh, what are you planning to do?' It wasn't the reaction he had expected from her.

'This.' He pulled her in close and kissed his wife on the lips. He then ripped up the letter.

'Are you sure?' Grace looked almost surprised by her husband's action.

'I don't think I'm finished with Whitby just yet.' He smirked.

Detective Matthews

Book 3

Coming Soon!

If you enjoyed this Detective Matthews novel please do consider leaving a small review on Amazon or Goodreads.

Thank you

Behind The Scenes

Even before the release of book one – The Planting of the Penny Hedge – I knew that Detective Matthews was going to be a multi-book series. I had multiple books plotted out, and had a time-line made for all the characters over the course of years to come (in their time line).

I have always talked about how research is such a huge part of my process – mostly because my books are set in the past – but another large part of my writing is planning. Especially when it comes to a series, I wanted to make sure I knew exactly why each character was in the story, and what their journey would look like. I am excited to tell these stories alongside the crimes that Matthews will be facing throughout the series.

After book ones released I found myself in a state of writer block. This was not the first time I had experienced this, but this time I found myself less inclined to wanting to break it. I thought I had fallen out of love with writing, and many times thought that I would walk away from it all together.

At the beginning of 2020 the Covid-19 pandemic hit the world hard, and despite this being a terrible time for so many people, it allowed me the time to breath and take note of what was important to me. I had not written in months by this point, and didn't think I wanted to. Shortly after the lockdown I came back to my writing, this time to write a new children's book – Olly The Top Security Dog – based on my real life dog. A book I had been eager to create for many years. Being a small book meant I wasn't overwhelmed with a large project, and there was no time frame set.

Olly's book was exatly what I needed to ease me back into my love of writing, and shortly after finishing it I turned my attention back to my first ever book – The Vintage Coat. This book was now five years old, and before my break I had started writing a diary style book – CHARLIE. Towards the end of 2020 I published CHARLIE along with an extended edition of The Vintage Coat.

After that I felt as though my writing mojo had returned, and I re-familiarized myself with Detective Matthews. Coming back to the character(s) felt like returning home, and I soon started writing The Regatta Murders, which was a joy. I hope you have enjoyed reading it, and look forward to the next one.

The Whitby Regatta

One thing I love about writing books in real places and time zones is that I can often include real events. The Whitby Regatta is one of the biggest calendar events in the town.

Originating in the 1840s, the Whitby Regatta is the oldest Regatta on the North East coast. What started with fishermen competing in their fishing boats, soon escalated into a larger event which drew thousands of spectators.

About The Author

Chris Turnbull was born in Bradford, West Yorkshire, before moving to Leeds with his family. Growing up with a younger brother, Chris was always surrounded by pets, from dogs, cats, rabbits and birds...the list goes on.

In 2012 Chris married his long term partner, since then Chris has relocated to the outskirts of York where he and his partner bought and renovated their first home together and spends his free time writing, walking his Jack Russell, Olly, and travelling as much as possible.

For more information about Chris and any future releases you can visit:

www.chris-turnbullauthor.com
facebook.com/christurnbullauthor
Twitter: @ChrisTurnbull20
Instagram.com/Chris.Turnbull20

Acknowledgements

I would firstly like to thank my long suffering husband, who as always is so supportive of my writing projects, and is constantly being handed the next chapter to read for feedback.

I would also like the thank Karen Sanders for doing an excellent job with the editing and proofreading, and making the process enjoyable.

I would like to thank Joseph Hunt for the fantastic book cover design, it has been great fun working with you on the three 'D' book covers and now the Detective Matthews series.

Lastly I would like to thank all the people who have read and enjoyed my books, it is an honour to read your reviews and see that you are enjoying what I do too.

Thank You!

The Vintage Coat 2020 Edition
Featuring added content, new chapters
& re-edited

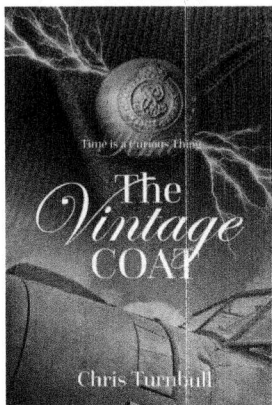

Joseph Michaels is 25 and an accidental time traveller.

After losing his job Joe finds himself working at the local second-hand shop. One day whilst unpacking new stock Joe comes across an old military coat that he just can't resist trying on.

Excited by the powers of the coat, Joe quickly takes it home where he discovers it allows him to travel between present day Alston, Cumbria and the same area during WWII.

Joe soon finds himself in the midst of living a double life. However, one night an unexpected air raid hits town and everybody is thrown into disarray; and Joe is faced with standing up for the ones he loves, even if it could cost him everything.

Charlie
A Prequel & Sequel to
The Vintage Coat

Available now on Amazon
Kindle & Paperback

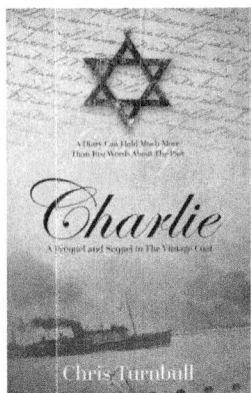